Nikki Logan li̶̶̶ ̶̶̶ ̶̶̶ ̶̶̶protected wetlands in We̶̶ ̶̶ ̶̶ ̶̶ith her long-suffering partner ̶̶ ̶̶ ̶̶agerie of furred, feathered and scaly ̶̶ ̶̶s. She studied film and theatre at university, and worked for years in advertising and film distribution before finally settling down in the wildlife industry. Her romance with nature goes way back, and she considers her life charmed, given she works with wildlife by day and writes fiction by night—the perfect way to combine her two loves. Nikki believes that the passion and risk of falling in love are perfectly mirrored in the danger and beauty of wild places. Every romance she writes contains an element of nature, and if readers catch a waft of rich earth or the spray of wild ocean between the pages she knows her job is done.

™

Mr Right
at the Wrong Time

Nikki Logan

All the characters in this book have no existence outside the imagination of the author, and have no relation whatsoever to anyone bearing the same name or names. They are not even distantly inspired by any individual known or unknown to the author, and all the incidents are pure invention.

First published in Great Britain 2012
by Mills & Boon, an imprint of Harlequin (UK) Limited.
Harlequin (UK) Limited, Eton House, 18-24 Paradise Road,
Richmond, Surrey TW9 1SR

© Nikki Logan 2012

ISBN: 978 0 263 89297 0

Harlequin (UK) policy is to use papers that are natural, renewable and recyclable products and made from wood grown in sustainable forests. The logging and manufacturing process conform to the legal environmental regulations of the country of origin.

Printed and bound in Spain
by Blackprint CPI, Barcelona

Also by Nikki Logan

Did you know these are also available as eBooks?
Visit www.millsandboon.co.uk

™

PROLOGUE

THE droning whine might have been coming from the tyres spinning in defiance of the absence of a solid surface beneath their tread, or from the still cooling engine, or from the air hissing from the deflating airbags.

Or quite possibly from deep inside Aimee Leigh's tight throat.

The brace of the steering wheel against her chest really didn't allow for much more than a whimper, followed rapidly by a shallow, painful breath, but making noise seemed like a priority because somewhere down deep Aimee knew that if she was making noise then she was still breathing. And if she was still breathing then she had something to save.

A life.

No matter how pathetic.

Adrenaline surged through her body as she flicked her eyes desperately left and right. It was pitch-black outside, except for a lone shaft of moonlight which fractured into a hundred different facets in the shattered windscreen of her little Honda. Long lengths of her hair brushed forward across her cheeks, defying gravity. She shook them just slightly, they swung in the open air, and the press of the steering wheel into her chest finally made some sense.

It wasn't pressing into her. She was pressing into it.

Down onto it.

Her world righted itself as she re-orientated and spidered her free hand along her middle to the pain in her abdomen—and discovered the seatbelt carving into her belly, straining against her weight, holding her in her seat.

Saving her life.

The moment she acknowledged it, its ruthless grip became unbearable. Her trembling fingers found the long cross length that was supposed to brace her from hip to shoulder—that had been until the force of the accident had pulled her free of it—and, forcing panic back, she squeezed her free arm up behind her and found the place where the seatbelt locked against its hidden reel. She curled her sticky fingers around it, got a good purchase, took as deep a breath as she could manage...

...and then she pulled.

Her whole body screamed as she forced her torso behind the fabric restraint and pressed herself back into the driver's seat. The release of pressure on her abdomen allowed a rush of blood into the lower half of her body, and it was only then that she realised she'd not been able to feel anything down there before. At all.

The painful burn of sensation returning kept her focused, and as she hung suspended at the waist and chest by her strong seatbelt she audited her extremities, made sure everything responded. But when she tried to flex her right foot an excruciating pain ripped up her leg and burst out into the night.

A bird exploded from its treetop roost just outside her shattered window, and as she slipped back into unconsciousness the urgent flap of its wings morphed in Aimee's addled mind into the hover of an angel.

A heavenly soul that had come to earth to act as midwife between her life...and her death.

CHAPTER ONE

'HELLO?'

The darkness was the same whether her eyes were open or closed so she didn't bother trying.

The disembodied voice that floated down to her made Aimee wonder if maybe she *was* dead, and she and her car and the tree she'd hit when she flew off the A10 had all been transported together in a tangled, inseparable mess into a void.

Some kind of spiritual waiting room.

Her heart battered against the seatbelt that still pinned her to the seat like an astronaut strapped into a shuttle.

Starved of light, her imagination lurched into overdrive. She replayed the slide and crash in her mind, each time making it worse and more violent. One minute she'd been travelling happily along through the towering eucalypts that defied gravity, growing forty-five degrees up out of the Tasmanian mountain all the way to the horizon…

…the next she'd been sliding and briefly airborne, before slamming into the trunk of this tree.

'Hello?'

Her head twitched slightly. Maybe her heavenly number was being called? She prised open her crusted, swollen lids and stared into the darkness that still reigned.

It didn't seem necessary to reply. Surely in the spirit world it would be enough just to think your response?

Yes. I'm here...

She reluctantly released her death-grip on her seatbelt and risked extending trembling fingers out into the dense nothing around her. They grazed against something solid almost immediately, and she traced them across the crusty, papery surface of bark, rolling tiny unbreakable cubes beneath her fingertips like reading Braille.

A tree branch. Riddled with pieces of her shattered windscreen.

She fumbled her touch to the roof of the car, found the interior light and—with only a momentary thought for what might be revealed—depressed the plastic panel and squinted at the sudden dim light.

Her dash had slipped forward about a foot, and buckled where parts of the engine had pushed into it. The roof above her had crushed downwards. But, most terrifying of all, an enormous tree limb had pierced the armour of her little car, through the windscreen and the passenger seat beyond it, and was taking much of the vehicle's weight. Aimee stared at the carnage and tasted the slide of salt down the back of her throat.

If that branch had come through just two feet closer…

The panic she'd been holding at bay so well these past hours surged forth. She plunged the car back into darkness, thicker and more cloying than before, and let the tears come. Crying felt good—it helped—and she let herself indulge because no one was around to see it. She'd never in her life cried in front of someone else, no matter the incentive, but what she did in the privacy of her own car wreck was her business.

'Can you hear me?'

The words just wouldn't quite soak into her overwhelmed, muddled mind, but the voice sounded angelic enough—deep and rich and… concerned. Shouldn't it be serene? Wasn't its job to reassure her? To set her mind and fears at rest and guide her to…wherever she was going? Glowing and transcendent and full of love.

'Make any kind of noise if you can hear me.'

A solitary beam of light criss-crossed back and forth from high above her, mother-ship-style, across the places her vehicle wasn't. It moved too fast for her fractured mind to make sense of what it revealed around her.

'Search and Rescue,' the voice said, sounding strained and uncomfortable and somehow closer. 'If you can hear me, make *any* kind of noise.'

For an angel, he was awfully demanding.

Aimee tried to speak, but her words came out as a creepy kind of gurgle. He didn't respond to her partial frog croak. She fumbled the hand that wasn't pinned behind her and found her car's horn, hoping to heaven she'd preserved enough battery.

She pressed.

And held.

The noise exploding through what had been so many hours of silence made her jump even though she knew it was coming, and her leg responded with sharp blades of protest. The long peal echoed through the darkness, sounding high and empty.

'I hear you,' the voice called back, sounding relieved and professional. 'I'll be with you soon. I'm just securing your car.'

A small lurch and a large clang were separated only by the barest of heartbeats, but then she felt and heard some of the weight of the car shift as whatever he'd used to secure it tightened into position. The move changed the dynamic of all the twisted fixtures in her front seat, and shifted some of the pressure of whatever had been pressing against her injured leg. It protested with violent sensation and she slammed her hand down on the horn again. Hard.

'Ho!' The voice yelled, then again urgently. Somewhere high above she thought she heard the word echo, but not in the same voice.

The tensioning stopped and the vehicle creaked and settled, more glass splintering from her windscreen and tinkling away into the night.

'Are you okay?' the voice yelled.

She swallowed back the pain and also wet her

throat. 'Yes,' she cried feebly, and then stronger, 'Yes. But my leg is trapped under the dash.' She hoped he'd do the maths and make the connection that their securing of the car was making her pain worse. She didn't have the energy or breath to explain.

'Got it.' She heard a thud on her roof but then nothing, no movement. Then some rustling outside the rear passenger side window. 'Any other injuries?' he called, closer. She heard the sounds of a mallet knocking something into place.

'Uh…I can't tell,' she whimpered.

'What's your name?' This time from somewhere over the top of her windscreen.

So they could advise her next of kin? Give her parents one more thing to fight over? she thought dismally. God, wouldn't they both make a meal of this? 'Aimee Leigh.'

He repeated that detail in short, efficient radiospeak to whoever he'd just called up to moments before. 'Are you allergic to morphine, Aimee?' he asked, definitely sounding close this time.

'I don't know.' And she didn't much care. The screaming of her leg had started to make every other part of her ache in sympathy.

'Okay…'

She heard more rustling from beyond the tree limb her Honda was skewered on and she craned her head towards the empty front passenger seat. Suddenly the darkness glowed into an ethereal white-blue light and a glow-stick seemed to levitate through the window, around the enormous branch, and then come to rest on the crippled dash of her car. She blinked her eyes in protest at the assault of blazing light. But as they adjusted the full horror of her situation came back to her. She looked at where her leg disappeared into the crumpled mess that had been her steering console, down at her right arm, which was wedged behind her between the seat and her driver-side door, then back again at the half-a-tree which stretched its grabbing fist past her into the back of her little hatchback.

But just as she tasted the rising tang of panic the man spoke again, from beyond the tree. 'How are you doing, Aimee? Talk to me.'

'I'm—' *A mess. Terrified. Not ready to die.* '—Okay. Where are you?'

'Right here.'

And suddenly a gloved hand reached through the leaves of the tree branch that had made a kebab out of her car and stretched towards her. It was heavy-duty, fluoro-orange, caked in old dirt and had seen some serious action. But it was beautiful and welcome, and as the fingers stretched towards her from the darkness Aimee reached out and wrapped all of hers around two of his. He curled them back into his palm and held on.

'Hi, Aimee,' the disembodied voice puffed lightly. 'I'm Sam, and I'll be your rescuer today.'

Right then—for the first time in hours—Aimee believed that she was actually going to make it.

Search-and-Rescue-Sam couldn't get close enough to do a visual inspection from outside the car, so he had her run through a verbal description of all her major body parts so he could try and assess her condition remotely. He seemed less concerned with her agonising leg than with the tightness in her chest, where her seatbelt bit, and with her forgotten arm—completely numb, immobile, and impossible for her to twist around to see.

'I don't like unknowns, Aimee Leigh,' he murmured as he ducked away to check the tension on the ropes holding the car in place. He kept up with the assessing questions and she kept her answers short and sharp—pretty much all her straining lungs would allow. The whole time he circled the vehicle, equipment clanking, and bit by bit she felt the car firming up in its position.

'I want to get a look at that arm if I can,' he said when he reappeared at the window beyond the tree limb.

'If I can't see it from here how are you going to see it from there?' she gasped.

'I'm not. I'm going to try and get in there with you.'

How? The two of them were separated by three feet of solid tree. And her door wasn't budging.

'Can you pop the hatch?'

She knew what he was asking—could she reach the door release?—but the request struck her as ludicrous, as if he wanted to load some groceries into the back of her brutalised car. She started to laugh, but it degenerated into a pained wheeze.

'Aimee? Hanging in there?'

Focus. He was working so hard to help her. 'I'm just...' She stretched her left arm across her body, to see if she could reach the release handle below her seat. She couldn't and, worse, she puffed like a ninety-year-old woman just from that. 'I'll have to take my seatbelt off...'

'No!'

The sudden urgency in his otherwise moderated voice shocked her into stillness, and she realised for the first time how hard he was working to keep her calm. He might be faking it one hundred percent, but it was working. Why the sudden urgency over her seatbelt? It had already done its job. It wasn't as if she could crash twice.

'I'll come through the back window. Shield yourself from the falling glass if you can.'

It took him a moment to work his way around to the back of the car. She followed his progress with her senses and pressed her good foot to the brake pedal until she could see his legs in her rearview mirror, splayed wide and braced on the failing tail-lights of her hatch, as though gravity meant nothing to him.

Somewhere at the back of her muddled mind she knew there was something significant about the fact that he'd abseiled down to her. But then she was thoroughly distracted by the realisation that he was going to come in there with her—put himself at risk—to help her. Anxiety burbled up in her constricted chest.

'Ready, Aimee? Cover your head.'

She curled her lone arm around her head and twisted towards the door. Behind her she heard a sharp crack, and then the high-pitched shattering of the back window. Tiny squares of safety glass showered down on her and pooled in the wrecked dash. She straightened and watched in the rear-view mirror as Sam folded down her back seats and lowered himself to where she was trapped.

A moment later he appeared between the two front seats of the car, bending uncomfortably around the sub-branches of the tree limb.

'Hey,' he said, warm and rich near her ear.

An insane and embarrassing sob bubbled up inside her at having rescue so close at hand—at having *him* so close at hand—and she struggled to swallow it back. 'I'm sorry...' she choked.

'Don't be. You're in an extraordinary situation. You wouldn't be human if you weren't scared.'

He didn't get it. How could he? She didn't feel scared. She felt stupidly safe. Just because he was here. And that undid her more than all the fear of the hours before he'd come. How long had it been since she felt so instantly *safe* with a man?

'Do you understand what's happened to you, Aimee?'

'I had an accident,' she squeezed out. 'I ran off the road.'

'Yeah, you did. Your car's gone down an embankment. The back is pressed into the hillside and the front has come to rest against a tree.'

'You make that sound so peaceful,' she whispered. The complete opposite of the violence that had befallen her and her car. She twisted around to see his face, but the angle was too tricky and it hurt too much to twist any further.

'Try not to move until I've stabilised your neck,' he murmured gently. He reached past her and adjusted the rearview mirror so that he could see her in it. And vice-versa. 'I want you to look at my eyes, Aimee. Focus.'

She lifted hers to the mirror and met his concerned, compassionate gaze, eyes crinkled at the edges from working outdoors, and the bluest blue she'd ever seen. At least she thought they were blue. They could have been any colour, given the emergency lighting was casting a sickly pallor over everything. He slid his finger up between them.

'Now, focus on my finger.' He moved it left and right, forward and back. She tracked the gloved finger actively in the mirror, but slipped once and went back to his eyes—just for a moment, for a better look. The most amazing eyes. Just staring at them made her calmer. And more drowsy.

'Okay.' He seemed satisfied.

'Did I pass?'

She lifted her head just slightly, so that the mirror caught the twist of his lips as he smiled.

'Flying colours. You're in pretty good shape for a girl wedged in a tree.'

She felt him brace his knees on the back of the front seats and heard him rifling through the kit he'd hauled in with him. 'I need to check you out physically, Aimee. Is that going to be okay?'

The man who'd climbed in here to rescue her? 'You can do…whatever you want.'

In her peripheral vision, in the dim glow of the cabin, she watched him strip off his gloves and twist a foam neck brace out of his bag.

'Just a precaution,' he said, before she could start worrying.

She let her head sag into the brace as he fitted it. Quite a comfortable precaution—if anything in this agonising situation could be called comfortable.

Next, he wedged a slimline torch between his teeth, and then he twisted through the gap between the driver and passenger seats, reaching for her legs. He held himself in place with one hand and dragged her torn skirt high up her thighs with the other. He pointed his torch down into the darkness at her feet, studying closely.

'I felt it break,' she said matter-of-factly—and softly, given how close his face was to hers—amazed that she could be calm at all. Still, what else could she do? Freaking out hadn't helped her earlier.

'It hasn't broken the skin, though,' he mumbled around the torch, sliding her dress modestly back into position. 'That's a good thing.'

He wasn't going to lie, or play down what was happening to her. She appreciated that.

'At least I can manage to break my leg the right way.' She winced. 'Wayne would be pleased.' One of very few things her dominating ex would have appreciated—or possibly noticed—about her.

Sam was eight-tenths silhouette, since the glow-stick was behind him on the dash but suddenly the front of the car was full of the smell of oil and leather, rescue gear and sweat, and good, honest man.

'Are you going to give me painkillers?' she said, to dislodge the inappropriate thought, and because everything was really starting to hurt now that the car was more stable and the pressure points had shifted.

'Not without knowing for sure you're not allergic. And not with the pain in your chest; you have enough respiratory issues without me compounding it with medication.'

'I hate pain,' she said.

His chuckle was totally out of place in this situation, but it warmed her and gave her strength. 'With the endorphins you'll have racing through your system you'll barely feel it,' he said, before twisting away to rifle in his bag again. When he returned he had a small bottle with him. 'But this will help take the edge off.'

She glanced sideways at the bottle. It didn't look very medical. She lifted her curious eyes to him in mute question rather than waste more breath on a pointless question.

'Green Ant Juice,' he said. 'It's a natural pain-killer. Aboriginal communities have used it for centuries.'

'What makes it juicy?'

His pause was telling. 'Better not to ask.'

Oh. 'Will it taste like ants?'

The rummaging continued. He resurfaced with an empty syringe. 'Have you tasted them?'

'I've smelled them.' The nasty, acrid scent of squashed ants.

Again the flash of white teeth in the mirror. 'Your choice. You prefer the pain?'

For answer, she opened her mouth like a young bird, and he syringed a shot of the sticky syrup into it. 'Good girl.'

His warm thumb gently wiped away a dribble of the not-quite-lemony juice that had caught on the corner of her lips. Her pulse picked up in re-sponse. Or it could have been the analgesic surg-ing into her system.

Either way, it felt good.

The gentle touch was so caring and sweet, while being businesslike, that it brought tears back to her eyes. When was the last time some-one had taken genuine care of her? Had just been there for her when it all went wrong? Her parents believed that prevention was infinitely better than the cure, and Wayne would have just rolled his eyes and scolded her for over-reacting.

As Sam withdrew his ungloved left hand her

eyes were tear-free enough to notice that his ring finger was bare and uniformly tanned. *Yeah, because that's always important to know in life or death situations.* She shook her head at her own subconscious. Her shoulder bit and she winced visibly.

'I'm going to have a look at your arm, Aimee. Just keep very still.'

She did—not that she could feel a thing; her arm had been wedged back there for so long it wasn't even bothering her, although obviously it was really bothering Sam. She heard and felt him changing positions, getting closer to her driver's door.

'Do you remember how the accident happened?' he asked, making conversation while he fiddled around behind her.

She shook her head. 'I was driving the A10. One minute everything was fine.' She filled her strained lungs again. 'The next I was sliding and then...' She shuddered. 'I remember the impact.' *Breath.* 'Then I passed out for a bit.' *Breath.* 'Then I woke up here in this tree. Stuck.'

Her strained respiration seemed unnaturally loud in the silence that followed. When he finally did speak he said, 'Looks like an oil patch on the asphalt. A local passing through slid on it, too, but managed to stop before the edge. He saw your tail-lights down here and called it in.'

Thank goodness he did. I might have been out here for days. Aimee lifted her chin to see better in the mirror what he was doing behind her. 'Sam, don't worry about whether it's going to hurt. Just do whatever you have to do. I'm a rip-the-Bandaid-off kind of girl, despite what I said earlier about pain.'

She felt his pause more than heard it. 'You can't feel this?'

The worry in his voice spiked her heart into a rapid flutter. 'I can't feel anything.'

When he spoke again, his voice was more carefully moderated. 'Your arm is wedged back here. I think it's dislocated. I've freed it up a little bit, and I'm going to try to push it forward, but this will go one of two ways. Either you won't feel a thing even once it's free—'

Meaning she might have damaged something permanently.

'—or the sensation is going to come back as soon as it's free. And if that happens it's going to hurt like hell.'

She felt a tug, but no pain. It was like having a numb tooth yanked. So far so good. 'Won't the ant juice help?'

'It won't have taken full effect—'

That was as far as he got. With a nasty crack her arm came free, and he pushed it forward back into the front seat where it belonged. The pain burst like white light behind her eyes, and came from her throat in an agonised retch as full sensation returned—arm burning, shoulder screaming.

His hands were at her hair instantly, stroking it back, soothing. 'That's the worst of it, Aimee.

It's all done now,' he murmured, over and over. 'All done…'

She rocked where she sat, holding her breath, damming back the tears, sucking the pain in, wanting so badly to be as brave as Sam was in coming down here for her. Then, as the ant juice and her own adrenaline kicked in, the rocking slowed and her body eased back in the seat, not fighting the restraint of the seatbelt as much.

'Better?' That voice again, warm and low just behind her. She lifted her eyes to the crooked rearview mirror, reached for it slowly with her good arm, missed and tried again through a slight fogginess. She adjusted it and found his eyes.

'Thank you,' she whispered, knowing it would never be enough, but just so grateful that she was no longer alone with her thoughts and fears of death.

He knew what she was saying. 'You're welcome. I'm sorry that hurt so much.'

'Not your fault. And it's easing off now.' If *easing off* could describe the deep, dull, throb coming from her right arm and leg. 'And it's made it easier to breathe. Talk.'

Though not perfectly.

'Don't get comfortable. We have a long way to go.'

'Is it time to get out?' God, she hoped so. Every time the car creaked and settled the breath was sucked out of her lungs.

The compassion turned to caution. 'Not just

yet. We have to wait for it to get a little bit lighter. It's not safe to try and haul you out in the dark.'

Given how unsafe she felt staying in, that was saying something. Although that wasn't strictly true; everything had got a whole heap less scary the moment Sam had first called out to her. But every minute she was here *he* was here, risking his life, too. 'You should go, then. Come back when it's morning.'

His eyes narrowed in the mirror. 'But you'd be alone.'

As uncomfortable as that thought made her, it was a heck of a lot more comfortable than something happening to him because of her. 'I've been alone most of the night. A few more hours won't kill me.' Except that it very well might, if things went wrong, her lurching stomach reminded her. But at least it would only be her. 'I don't want you to get hurt because of me.'

The crinkles at the corners of his eyes multiplied. 'I appreciate the thought, but I know what I'm doing.'

'But the hatch isn't open.' So if the car slipped further it wouldn't just slide away from around him, and the harness she guessed tethered him to something above them. It would take him, too. And who knew how steep this embankment was.

'We're secure enough.'

'Do you do this for a living?' Suddenly she wanted to know. What kind of person risked his life for total strangers? Plus talking took her mind off…everything else.

'Amongst other things, yes.'

She tipped her head and spoke more freely than she might have without fifty mils of squished ants zooming through her blood. 'Are you an adrenaline junkie?'

He laughed and checked her pulse, his fingers warm and sure at the base of her jaw under the foam neck brace. Her heart kicked up its pace.

'A little fast…' he murmured to himself, then turned his focus back to her. 'No, I'm not interested in risk-taking for the sake of it. But to save someone's life…'

'I don't want you risking your life for mine.'

Blue eyes held hers in the mirror. 'Why not?'

'Because…' *it wasn't worth it* '…this was my mistake. You shouldn't have to pay for it.'

He looked like he wanted to argue. 'Well, if I do my job right then neither of us will be paying. Excuse me a sec.'

He reached to his collar and pressed a button she'd only just noticed. He had a speedy conversation with whoever was on the other end of the radio at his hip. It was mostly coded medical talk, but she read his thin lips and his deep frown well enough.

'Assess this as Code Three. Will offer hourly sit-reps.' More distant crackles, then his eyes lifted to hers in the mirror and held them as he spoke, a fatal resignation written clearly in them. 'Negative, Topside. Requiring static again. We've just gone Code Two.'

After not much more communication he

signed off, and the silence that followed was the longest that had fallen since he'd scrambled into her beleaguered Honda. When he finally did speak, it was hushed.

He cleared his throat. 'If anyone asks, you passed out just then.'

Her eyebrows shot up. 'Did you just lie?'

'Would you feel better if I said I save them up for very important moments?'

I'd feel better if you didn't do it at all. Her father was a liar, and she didn't like even the slightest connection between the two men in her mind.

She raised both brows for answer. Wow, when had she got so confident? One month ago she never would have challenged someone like this. Driving off a mountain really brought out the best in a girl.

Plus, with Sam, she felt safe expressing herself. On five minutes' acquaintance.

He sighed and relented at her pointed look. 'It seems I'm the only one who thinks I'm better off down here with you,' he said.

'Were you ordered to go back up? Why?'

He considered her in the mirror. Now that her arm was free she could twist her body further around. She did it now, turning to face him for the first time, though it hurt to do it. Her already tight breath caught further.

She hadn't imagined it… Piece by piece in the mirror she'd thought he was intriguing. Fully assembled he was gorgeous. There was something almost…leonine…about the way his features all came together. Dark, high eyebrows over blue almond-shaped eyes. Defined cheekbones, trigger jaw. All with a coat of rugged splashed over the top. As if she wasn't breathy enough…

'Why, Sam?'

His mind worked furiously and visibly. 'Okay…' He resettled himself into the gap between the seats and lowered his voice. As if he was about to share a great secret. As if there was anyone but them here to hear it.

'We're not just resting against a tree, Aimee. Or on a hillside.'

She appreciated his use of the collective. 'We' sounded so much better than 'you' when someone was breaking bad news. And he was. His whole body confessed it.

'Where are we?' she whispered, glancing out at the inky blackness around them and remembering how she'd imagined earlier that it was death's waiting room. But as she said the words she realised… He'd abseiled down to her. And when she'd first tried to move her leg and screamed a bird had exploded from its roost *right next to her window,* not high above it. And she'd heard her wheels spinning freely in space when she'd first slammed to a stop.

Her heart lurched.

'Or should I be asking *how high* are we?'

CHAPTER TWO

SHE saw the truth in the flinch of his dark brows. A tight pain stabbed high in her chest. She was so, *so* bad with heights. 'Oh, my God…'

'Aimee, stay calm. We're secure. But we don't know what damage the impact has done to the tree—if any. That's the unknown.'

She stared at him. 'You hate unknowns?'

His eyes grew serious. 'Yeah. I do.'

'But you're in here.'

'I've made it safe.'

But still he was refusing to leave her. 'You have to go.'

'No.'

'Sam—'

'It's going to get light in a couple of hours,' he pushed on, serious. 'I want to be here when that happens.'

For the rescue? Or for when she could see what was below them—or wasn't—and went completely to pieces? She shifted her focus again and stared out through her shattered, flimsy windscreen, partially held together only by struggling tint film. The only thing stopping her from falling into—and through—that windscreen was her seatbelt.

She turned back to stare at him again. In truth she really, horribly, desperately didn't want to be alone. But she didn't want him hurt, either. Not the man who'd taken such gentle care of her.

'Don't even worry about it, Aimee,' he said, before she'd even finished thinking it through. 'It's not your choice to make. It's mine.'

'I don't get a say?'

'None. I'm in charge in this vehicle. It's my call.'

I'm in charge. How many years had she secretly rebelled against 'in charge' men. Men who thought they knew what was best for her and insisted on spelling it out. Her father. Wayne. Men who liked her better passive, like her mother. Yet here she was crumbling the moment an honest-to-goodness *'take charge'* man told her what to do.

But, truthfully, she didn't want to be alone. Not for one more moment of this ordeal.

'So, what do we do until it gets light?' she asked.

'I'll keep monitoring your condition, make sure the car's still sound. I can radio up for anything you need.'

Silence fell. 'So we just…talk?'

'Talking is good. I don't want you dropping off to sleep.'

But making small talk seemed wrong under

the circumstances. And it was just too much of a reminder that she didn't know him at all, despite the strange kind of intimacy that was forming between them. A bubble she didn't particularly want to burst.

'What do we talk about?'

'Anything you want. I'm told I'm good company.'

She glanced up into the mirror in time to see him flick his eyes quickly away. Maybe this was awkward for him, too.

She scratched around for something to say that wasn't about the weather. Something a bit more meaningful. Something that would normalise this crazy situation. 'You said Search and Rescue is only part of your job. What's the other part?' With every minute that passed, her breath was coming more easily.

He seemed unused to making conversation with his rescuees, but he answered after just a moment. 'I'm a ranger for Tasmania's Parks and Wildlife Service.'

The man who abseiled down rockfaces to save damsels in distress also looked after forests and the creatures in them. *Of course he did.* 'So this is just moonlighting for you?'

He chuckled, and shone the small torch on the fixings of her seatbelt. 'Don't worry. They sent me because I'm the best vertical rescue guy in the district. We don't get enough demand for a full time Search and Rescue team up here.'

'Small mercies.'

He sat back. 'True.'

'Which do you enjoy more?'

His eyes lifted back to hers in the mirror, held them in his surprise. Had no one ever asked him that? 'Hard to say. Search and Rescue is more... tangible. Immediate. But the forests need a champion, too.'

'This part has got to be more exciting, though?' Her dry tongue had made a mess of that sentence.

Sam rummaged in his equipment for a moment, before reappearing between the seats with a sponge soaked in bottled water. He pressed it to her lips and Aimee sucked at it gratefully.

'It's not the excitement I'm conscious of.' He frowned as she sucked. 'Though that's how it is for some of my colleagues. For me it's the importance.' He withdrew the sucked-dry sponge and resaturated it. 'I think I'd feel the same way if it was national secrets I was protecting. Or a vial of some rare cells instead of a person.'

The ants' innards were making her feel very rubbery and relaxed, and the water had buoyed her spirits. She chuckled, low and mellow. 'Just in case I was beginning to feel special.'

He smiled at her. 'Right now you're very special. There's sixteen trained professionals up there—all here for you.'

The scale of the rescue operation came crashing into focus for her. That was sixteen people who should be home in bed, wrapped around their loved ones. 'I'm so sorry—'

'Aimee, don't be. It's what we do.'

Did Sam have someone like that at home? Someone worrying about him when he was out? She could hardly ask that question, so she asked instead, 'How many lives have you saved?'

He didn't even need to count. 'Twenty-seven. Twenty-eight after today.'

Aimee's eyebrows shot up, and she turned in her seat as best she could. Her shoulder bit cruelly. His hand pressed her back into stillness gently.

'*Twenty-seven!* That's amazing.' Then she looked more closely at him. At the shadows in his gaze. 'How many have you lost?'

'I don't count the losses.'

Rubbish. Everyone counted the losses. It was human nature. 'Meaning, *"I'm not about to tell a woman trapped in her car whether or not I saved the last woman trapped in her car"*?'

His smile was gentle. 'Meaning I don't like to think about it.'

No. She could understand that. Given how much of a partnership this rescue was, she could only imagine how he'd feel when he couldn't save someone. Maybe someone he'd bonded with. Like they were bonding now. She smiled tightly. 'Well, on behalf of all women everywhere trapped in their cars I'd like to say thank you for trying. We can't ask for more.'

Ridiculously, just acknowledging that she wasn't the first person who'd been in a life-or-death situation made her feel just a little bit more in control of this one. Other people had survived to tell their tales.

In control. A further novelty. She frowned. *How bad had she let things get?*

'Sure you can. You can ask me for whatever you need right up until they're loading you into the back of the ambulance. Then I know I've done everything I can.'

'Putting yourself at so much risk. It must be hard on...' *Your family. Your girlfriend.* Was she seriously going to start obsessing on his avail-ability? It seemed so transparent. Not to mention hideously inappropriate. In that moment she de-termined not to even hint for more information about his personal life. 'Hard on you...emotion-ally.'

He thought about that. 'The benefits outweigh the negatives or I wouldn't do it.'

He reached forward to check her pulse again and she studied the line of his face. There was more to it than that, she was sure. But it would be rude to dig. His fingers brushed under her jaw for the third time and her already tight breath caught further.

'Would my wrist be easier?' she asked, lifting her good arm because it felt like the appropriate thing to do.

He shook his head and pressed tantalisingly into the skin just down from her ear, monitoring his watch. 'You have a nice strong pulse there.'

And it gets stronger every time you brush those fingers along my throat.

'Aimee...?' She looked at him sideways, her lashes as low as his voice. His smile was half twist, half chuckle. 'Don't hold your breath—it affects your pulse.'

Heat surged up her throat around his fingers. Wow. Did ant juice turn everyone into a hormone harlot?

Fortunately he misread her flush. 'Don't feel awkward. I'm trained for this, but I'm guessing this is your first major incident.'

She nodded. 'I've never even been to hospital.'

'Never?'

She grasped at the normal topic of conversation. 'Not counting my birth.'

'Are you super-healthy or just super lucky?'

'A little of both. And it helps when your parents won't let you lift so much as a box without assistance.' The same as every man she'd dated. 'It's hard to hurt yourself falling out of a tree when they are all off-limits. And streams. And streets.'

'Protective, huh?'

'You could say that.' Or you could say her parents were competitive and bitter after their divorce and neither of them wanted to give the other the slightest ammunition. 'They both went a bit overboard in protecting me.' She'd grown up thinking that was normal. 'It wasn't until I left home that I realised other kids were allowed to make mistakes.'

'How old were you when you left home?'

'Twenty-two.'

'So you get points for taking the initiative and getting out of there?'

It hadn't been easy to break away from both of them so, *yeah,* she did get points.

But then she lost them again for leaping out of the frypan into the fire with a nightmare like Wayne.

'Anyway, it's just as well my parents aren't here to see this,' she joked. 'They'd have me locked up for ever and never let me leave the house.' *Or they'd have each other in court trying to score points off me.*

'Give them credit for getting you this far in one piece,' he murmured.

She laughed, and then winced at the pain. 'If you don't count the broken leg and dislocated shoulder. And the bruised sternum.'

'Don't forget the gash on your forehead.'

Really? Her hand slid up and followed the trail of stickiness down to her lashes. That explained the stinging in her eyes earlier. Lord, what must she look like? Black and blue and with the fine white powder from three airbags all over her? She wanted to check in the mirror, but that just smacked of way too much vanity. And it was too close to publicly declaring her interest in whether or not Sam was looking at her as *her*…or just as a person to be rescued.

'Here…' he said, curling between the seats again and bringing his face closer to hers. He efficiently swabbed at the superficial cut with a damp medicated wipe, and then fixed the two sides of the wound together with butterfly tape. Then he gently swabbed up some of the dried blood that ran down over her brow. Aimee stole a chance to breathe in some of his air.

'You'll be back to beautiful in no time,' he said.

The temptation to stare at his eyes close-up was overwhelming, but it seemed too intimate suddenly so she shifted her focus lower, to his lips, before forcing them away for something less gratuitous. Which was how she ended up staring at a freckle just left of his nose while he ministered to her wound.

Freckle-staring seemed suitably modest.

Awkwardness tangled in amongst the awareness suddenly zinging between them, and she struggled for something harmless to say. 'I can honestly say that's the first time anyone has ever said that to me. Especially by the dying light of a glow stick.'

A deep frown cut his handsome face immediately as he seemed to realise that the iridescent emergency light had dimmed to something closer to a sickly, flickering candlelight. He stared at it as though he couldn't quite believe he'd failed to notice, then disappeared into the back to rummage in his bottomless kit.

'It's got nothing to do with the colour in your cheeks,' he said, snapping a second glow-stick to activate the chemicals inside, and reaching forward to place it next to the first. Las Vegas light filled the car, and for a heartbeat the tree outside the windscreen, but the graduated darkness beyond it that didn't show a hint of ground.

Aimee swallowed hard.

'Look at how you're handling yourself,' he said. 'You're very calm, under the circumstances.'

She captured his eyes in the mirror. 'It just means I'm good at denial. It doesn't mean I'm not afraid.'

He stilled, and the intensity in his gaze reached right through the glass of the mirror and twisted around her lungs, preventing them from expanding. 'I'm not leaving you, Aimee.'

'I know,' she squeezed out.

'We'll be out in a couple of hours.'

'Uh-huh.' But it sounded false even to her own ears.

'You don't believe me?'

'I want to. I really do.'

'Do you trust me?'

Did she? She'd believed every single thing he'd said. She'd done every single thing he'd asked, without question, and not just because he'd pulled rank on her. Sam was trained, capable and compassionate, and he'd not done anything to earn her distrust. Even though she'd known him less than an hour she felt a more natural connection with him than some of the people she'd known her whole life.

Wow. That was a bit sad.

'I do trust you,' she whispered. But he'd have no way of knowing how rare that was.

'Then trust I'll get you out of here.'

She looked at him long and hard. 'I know you want to.'

'And I always get what I want.'

As a kid, she'd practised for weeks to teach herself the one-eyebrow lift and she did it now, desperate to retreat from the chemistry swirling smoke-like around them. The butterfly tape over her left brow tugged slightly. 'Such confidence.'

'I don't start something without finishing it. It's a point of principle.'

So how had he coped with those people he'd not been able to save? Maybe sitting in vehicles like this one with them, knowing he'd failed? Her heart ached for the memories he must have. But she wasn't about to ask. For his sake…and hers.

She shivered convulsively. 'Did the temperature just drop?'

'Hang on…' He disappeared for a moment and then squeezed back through the gap with a tightly rolled silver tube. It unfolded into an Aimee-sized foil blanket. Together they tucked it around her as best they could. Down over her good leg. Carefully around her injured arm.

Sam stroked back her hair from the neck brace with two fingers and tucked a corner of the blanket in behind her shoulder. Heat surged where he touched and became trapped beneath the insulation. A perverse little voice wondered if it would be inappropriate to ask him to touch her every ten minutes, to keep the heat levels optimum. She might as well get some use out of the unexpected chemistry between her and her knight-in-shining-fluoro. His heat soaked into her chilled skin.

'God, that's good...' Her good hand was outside the blanket, and she used it to tuck the foil tightly under her thighs to seal more warmth in.

'Don't cover your injured leg,' he said, withdrawing back between the seats. 'The cold is actually good for it.' Then, without asking, he reached forward and took her exposed hand between his and started to rub it. Vigorously. Impersonally. Creating a friction heat that soaked into her icy fingers and wrist. He did the same up and down her bare arm.

'How's that?' he murmured.

Heavenly. And it had nothing to do with the blanket. 'Better.'

He rubbed in silence as the insulation from the foil sheet did its job. But as the minutes went by his businesslike rubbing slowed and turned into a hybrid of a massage and a hold. Just cupping her smaller hand between his own like a heated human glove.

'So...' The unease with which he paused made her wonder whether there was still more bad news to come. 'Is there...anyone you'd like us to call for you? Your parents?' He glanced down at the fingers he held within his own. 'A partner?'

She frowned. Absolutely not Wayne. They were well and truly over. And she'd prefer to call her parents from the safety of terra-firma, when they wouldn't have to see the immediate evidence of what heading off alone into the wilds had done to her and when they'd have less reason to tear each other to pieces. Work wouldn't miss her for days yet—they knew how she got when she got to the transcribing stage of a project. 'No. Not if you truly believe we'll make it.'

'We'll make it.' His certainty soaked through her just like his body heat. 'But is there someone you'd call if you thought you *weren't* going to make it?'

'Hedging your bets, Sam?' Maybe that was wise. She still had to get hauled out of here successfully.

His lips twisted. 'It would be wrong of me not to ask.'

Danielle? That would get a tick in the friend box and the work box at the same time. She folded her brows and tried to make her foggy brain focus…

'It's not like prison, Aimee. You can have more than one phone call.' Then he looked closer. 'Or none at all. It's not compulsory.'

How pathetic if she couldn't even identify one *'in case of emergency'* person. And how ridiculous. She sighed. 'My parents, probably.'

He pulled a small notepad from his top pocket. 'Want to give me a number?'

She stared at him, and then to the floor of the passenger seat. 'Their numbers are in my phone.'

He blinked at that. 'You don't know your parents' phone numbers?'

'I have them on speed dial.' There was no way

that didn't sound defensive. Not when she knew how little wear those two buttons actually got.

'How about a name and address, then?'

There was no judgement there, yet his words somehow reeked of it. She glared and provided the information; he jotted it down, then called it up to all those people waiting up top. Waiting for sunrise. They confirmed, and promised to make contact with her parents. She wanted to shout out so they'd hear her: *Wait until seven. Dad hates being woken.* Sam held the earpiece out so she could hear their acknowledgement.

Then they both fell into uncomfortable silence. It stretched out endlessly and echoed with what he wasn't saying.

She pressed back against her seat. 'Go ahead, Sam. Just say it. We can't sit here in silence.'

'Say what?'

'Whatever's making you twitch.'

Even with full permission, and all the time in the world to tell her what he thought, Sam refrained. It was sad how surprised she was about that. Men in her life didn't usually withhold their opinions. Or their judgement. Not even for a moment.

'I watched my parents raise my brothers and sisters. Eighty percent of it was guesswork, I reckon. Parents don't get a manual.'

She shook her head. 'You're from a big family?'

He nodded. 'And my folks got a whole lot

more right with my younger brothers than with me, so maybe practice makes perfect?'

'What did they get wrong with you, Search-and-Rescue-Sam?' He seemed pretty perfect to her. Heroic, a good listener, smart, gentle fingers, and live electricity zinging through his blood-stream...

'Oh-ho... Plenty. I made their lives hell once I hit puberty.'

She studied him. 'I can see you as a heart-breaker with the girls.'

He smiled. 'No more than your average teen. But I was a handful, and I ran with some wild mates.'

'Another thing I don't have trouble seeing.' Maybe it was the uniform. Maybe it was the torn-out-of-bed-at-midnight stubble. Maybe it was the glint in those blue eyes. He had the bad-boy gene for sure. Just a small one. Not big enough to be the slightest bit off-putting but just big enough to be appealing. Dangerously appealing.

'Fortunately my older brother intervened, and turned me into the fine, upstanding citizen you see before you.'

She laughed, and her spirits lifted a hint more. Insane and impossible, but true enough. She shifted in her seat to remind herself of where they were and how much danger they were still in. 'Tell me about him. I'm sick of talking about me.'

And of thinking about the wrong turns she'd made in her life.

'Tony's two years older than me. The first. The best.'

'Is that your parents' estimation or yours?'

He looked at her. 'Definitely mine. He was everything I wanted to be growing up. The full hero-worship catastrophe.'

She smiled. 'I can't imagine having siblings.'

'I can't imagine not.'

'You want kids? In the future?' she added, in case her breathless question sounded too much like an offer.

He shrugged. 'Isn't that why we're here? As a species, I mean? I like my genes, I'd like to see what else could be done with them.'

She was starting to like his genes, too. Very much. He had a whole swag of good-guy genes to go with the bad-boy one. And the dreamy eyes. Silence fell, and she realised into what personal territory they'd strayed. She was practically interviewing him for the job of future husband. 'Sorry. Occupational hazard. I get way too interested in people's lives.'

'Why? What do you do?'

'I'm a historian. Oral History. For the Department of Heritage.'

'You talk to people for a living?'

'I swing between talking endlessly to people and then spending weeks alone pulling their stories into shape.'

'What for?'

'So they're not lost.'

'I mean what happens with them?'

She shrugged. 'They get archived. Locked away somewhere safe.'

'No one ever hears them?'

'Sure they do. Every story is catalogued by topic and theme and subject, so they can be accessed by researchers into just about anything anywhere in the world.'

'Do you get to see the end results?' he asked.

'Not usually. Just my own research.'

'So your work just goes on file somewhere? To gather dust, potentially, if no one ever looks for it?' he mused.

'Potentially.' She shrugged. 'You think something's missing from that equation?'

'Isn't it a bit…thankless?'

She stared at him, wondering if he realised what he'd just revealed. Search-and-Rescue-Sam liked to be appreciated. This was exactly why she loved to do what she did. For the moments a person let a bit of his true self slip.

She smiled. 'Not at all. Our jobs aren't too dissimilar.'

He frowned at her.

'We both save lives. You preserve their flesh for another few decades,' she said. 'I preserve their stories for ever. For their family. For perpetuity. There's more to people's time on earth than genetics.'

Which was why it was such a crime that her life was only just beginning at the ripe old age of twenty-five. She'd wasted so much time.

He considered her. 'So what's your story,

Aimee Leigh? What are you doing up here in the highlands?'

'Working. I've just finished a history, and the next few weeks I'll be pulling it all together.' She glanced around. 'Or I would have been.'

'You always do that in remote parts of the state?'

'I wanted some time alone. I rented a house at Brady's Lake.'

His eyebrows lifted. 'How's that time alone working out for you?'

Laughing felt too good. She went on longer than was probably necessary, and ended in a hacking cough. Sam reached out and slid his warm fingers to her pulse again, counting, then saying, 'Nothing makes you reassess your life quite like nearly losing it.'

True enough. She'd planned on doing some serious soul-searching while up in the highlands and really getting to grips with how she'd let others run her life for so long. She refused to think it was because she wasn't capable.

Well, she'd wanted space to think and she'd got it. Above, below and on both sides.

The pause fell again. But then she had a thought. 'Can you see my handbag, Sam?'

He looked around. 'Where is it?'

'It was on the passenger seat.' Not any more.

'What do you need? Your wallet?'

'That's all replaceable. But I have someone's life in there.'

'The person whose history you were about to start working on?'

She nodded. 'All my notes on a thumb drive.'

'I'll have a look,' he said. 'Not like I have somewhere else to be.'

He wedged himself between the seats again, but twisted away from her this time, bracing his spread knees on the seat backs and reaching out for the glow-stick. The yellow light moved with him as he stretched down towards the floor of the passenger seat.

But as he did so the car lurched.

'Sam!' Aimee screamed, just as his two-way radio burst into a flurry of activity. But the sudden splintering pain from her chest crippled her voice.

He froze in position and then slowly retreated, his strong muscles pulling him back up, bringing the light with him. He spoke confidently into the transmitter at his collar, but his words were three-parts buzz to Aimee. Her heart hammered so hard against her chest wall she was sure it might just split open.

She might have caused them to go crashing to the ground—who knew how far below? For a handbag! For a story! Tears filled her eyes.

'Sorry, Aimee,' he said, breathing heavily and righting himself more fully. 'I'll get it when the car's hauled up.'

She shook her head, unable to speak, unable to forgive herself for putting them both at such risk.

He looked more closely at her. 'Aimee? Were you hurt? Is the pain back?'

She shook her head—too frightened to speak—though her burst of activity had definitely got her pain receptors shrieking.

'I wouldn't have tried that if I'd thought it would actually dislodge us. That was just a settle. It will probably happen again whether we move or not. It doesn't mean we're going to fall.'

Tell her clenched bladder that. She nodded quickly. Still too scared to move more than a centimetre.

He found her eyes in the mirror. 'Aimee, look at me.'

She avoided his eyes, knowing what she'd just done. *Get my handbag, Sam...* As though they were just sitting here waiting for a bus. Maybe her parents were right not to trust her with important decisions.

'At *me*, Aimee.'

Finally she forced her focus to the mirror, to the blue, blue eyes waiting for her there. They were steady and serious, and just so reliable it was hard not to believe him when he spoke. 'We're thoroughly wedged between the tree and the rockface, and tethered to a three-tonne truck up top. We won't be square-dancing any time soon, but you don't need to fear moving. *We are not going to fall.*'

She looked at the rugged cut of his jaw and followed it down to the full slash of his lips, then up to his strong, straight nose and back to his eyes. Every part of him said *reliable*. Capable. Experienced. And a big part of her responded to the innate certainty in his manner. But an even bigger part of her was responding to something else. Something more fundamental. The something that would never have let him get this close, this quickly under her skin, if not for the fact that the fates had thrown them together like this. She would have followed him out onto the bonnet of her car with no safety harness if he'd asked her to with the kind of sincerity and promise that he was throwing at her right now in the mirror.

And extraordinary as it was, given how slow she was to trust strangers, she realised why.

She believed in him.

'We are not going to fall,' he'd said. She nodded, letting her breath out on a long, controlled hiss.

But deep down she feared that while that might be true literally, she could see herself falling very easily for a man like Sam. And just as hard.

Under these circumstances, that was a very, very bad idea.

CHAPTER THREE

'So who's Wayne?'

Aimee's head came up with a snap as Sam shifted again behind her. He was a big guy, and he had squeezed himself into the small space left vacant by the tree branches in the back of her little car and been settled there for over an hour.

'Wayne?'

'You mentioned his name earlier. Boyfriend? Brother?'

Was this conversation or curiosity? 'Ex.'

'Recent ex?'

'Recent enough. Why?'

'There was a…certain tone in your voice when you mentioned him.'

'A certain sarcastic tone?'

She heard the smile in his voice. 'Possibly.'

Aimee shifted back in her seat. Wayne was not someone she usually liked to talk about, liked even to *think* about, but all bets were off in this surreal setting. Their physical proximity demanded it. 'Wayne and I turned out not to be a good fit.'

'I'm sorry.'

'Don't be. I'm not. I'd rather have found out now than later.' And it was true—no matter how challenging she'd found it to walk away. Even though he'd been giving her clear signals that she was somehow deficient in his eyes. Even though she knew he wasn't good for her. She'd wriggled out from under the controlling thumbs of her parents only to fall prey to a man just like them at a time when she was most susceptible to him. 'If I'd put any longer into the relationship I might have been more reluctant to end it.'

Another long pause. Funny how she'd only known Sam a handful of minutes but she already knew how to tell a thinking pause from an awkward one. This was thinking.

'Not everyone finds that strength,' he finally said.

'You learn a thing or two recording life histories for a living. About achievements. About regrets. I don't want any regrets in my life.'

She'd lost him again. His eyes stared out into the darkness.

What was *his* story?

'Sam,' she risked, after a comfortable silence had stretched out, 'any chance you can lower the back of my seat a bit? Safely?' She didn't want a repeat of what happened before.

He studied the angle of the car and her position in it. His answer was reluctant. 'The seatbelt is working well right now specifically because it's nearly at ninety degrees.'

'Even just a little bit? It's doing my head in, looking straight down, wondering what's down there, knowing that I'd crash straight through if the seatbelt gave.'

His hand slipped onto her shoulder through the gap between the seats. 'The seatbelt is what's keeping your body from putting too much weight on your bad leg.'

Oh.

Her disappointment must have reached him, though, because he said a moment later, 'Let me just try something.' He rummaged in his kit again, and then emerged with a set of flex-straps.

Aimee chuckled tightly. 'You got a decaf latte in that Tardis, Doctor?'

He smiled as he wrapped one strap carefully around her waist and fixed it behind the seat, then the other under her good shoulder and hooked it on the headrest. 'These aren't generally for people, but I'll be gentle with them.'

He pulled the two together and clipped one end of a climbing tether onto it, then fixed the other end to his own harness. If she fell she'd snag on his safety rope. Or pull him down with her.

That was a cheery thought!

'Ready?'

So ready. So *very* ready not to be facing death literally head-on for every minute of this ordeal. She felt him fumbling along the edge of her seat for the recline lever and then suddenly the back of the seat gave slightly—just slightly—and he lowered it halfway to a fully reclined position.

She hung on to her seatbelt lifeline and prepared for the pain of more of her body weight hitting her leg, but the flexi-straps did their job and held her fast to the seat-back. It really wasn't too bad.

'Oh, thank you.' Her view was now the buckled roof of the car. A thousand times better than hanging out over who knew what. 'Thank you, Sam.'

With her seat now reclined into the limited free space in the back of the car, there was nowhere for him to go but into the expanded gap between the front seats. He wedged himself there, with his spine to the passenger seat back, his shoulder pressing against the branch, facing her across the tiny gulf he'd opened up.

Unexpected bonus. She could talk to him front on.

'You look funny,' she said softly. *Though still gorgeous.* 'Your face is back to front without the mirror.'

'You look good.' He smiled, then flushed as she dropped her eyes briefly. 'I just meant that pretty much everything on you is intact. I can't tell you what a relief it was to find that. Just to hear you honk that damned horn.'

Aimee sobered. He must hold some truly terrible images in his head.

'It's always the calmest most compliant people that have the worst injuries. They're the ones I dream about later.' He tucked her foil covering back in, keeping up his part of the conversation. She let his deep, rich voice wash over her. 'It's the guy with a twisted ankle and a golf tournament to get to that makes life hell. We've had hikers activate their EPIRB halfway up a mountain because they're tired and want a lift back down.' He shook his head.

'Where do I fall on that scale?' Was she being too high maintenance? *Get my handbag, Sam. Lower my seat, Sam...*

'You have a scale all your own. All the reason in the world to be losing it, but holding up pretty well all things considered.'

She was—and that was really saying something, given her upbringing. Where the heck would she have learned resilience from in her bubblewrap childhood? But honour made her confess. 'I was sobbing my heart out before I heard you calling.'

That seemed to genuinely pain him. 'I'm sorry I didn't get to you quicker. We had to assess the safety.'

She pinned him with her gaze. 'I'm so glad you found me at all. Imagine if you hadn't.' It hit her then, for the first time, how long, slow and awful her death would have been. She swallowed back a gnarled lump and just stared, watching the play of emotion running over his features. Sadness. Regret. Confusion. But then his eyes lifted and it was just…light. And it changed him.

'How old are you, Sam?'

'Thirty-one.'

'How is it that a man like you who wants children doesn't yet have any?' That was the closest she'd come to asking him outright: *Why are you still single?*

His eyes grew wary, but he finally answered. 'It takes one to want it but two to make it a reality.'

'You don't have women knocking down your door to help you along with that reality? You're gorgeous.'

His eyes grew cautious. But they didn't dull. On the contrary, they filled with a rich sparkle. 'Are you offering?'

She held her breath. Tilted her head. 'Are you flirting?'

The bright sparkle in his eyes immediately dimmed. The smile straightened out into a half-frown.

Her breath caught. 'You are.'

'Sorry. Really inappropriate. Just playing to my strengths.'

His confusion touched her. 'Don't apologise. I'm battered and broken and feeling pretty average. It made me smile.'

'I'm glad I could make you smile, then.'

'Do they train you for that?' she asked pertly.

'For what?'

'Keeping up people's spirits with a sexy smile.'

The hint of colour high in his jaw brought her back to her senses. The man was just trying to keep her alive. He would say just about anything. Flirting included. It probably *was* in his training manual. Which meant it had to end. One of them had to put things back on a more real footing.

She took a deep breath. 'Sorry, Sam. I think that was the ant juice talking. I apologise.'

He brushed it off with a shake of his head. 'It's not generally known for its truth serum properties.'

A blush stole up her cheeks, but this time he was staring straight at her. There was no hiding it. 'A crazy side-effect?'

'It's probably written on the bottle somewhere. *"May cause outbursts of inappropriate confession."'*

A gentleman, too. Handing her as dignified an exit as she was going to get. 'Thank you. For keeping me sane.' *For keeping things light.*

'That's how this works. You're the victim. Whatever you need…'

Victim. The word put an early end to the golden glow of promise that had filled her from the inside out at his gentle teasing. Wasn't that exactly what Danielle had accused her of being? By letting her father and Wayne run her life and others control her career? That hadn't been a fun conversation. But it had been necessary. It had triggered the rapid departure of Wayne from her life and this journey of self-discovery. 'Is that what I am?'

He stared at her—hard. 'No. You're brave and open and the least victim-like victim I've ever met.'

'It's because you're with me. I'd be a basket case without you here.'

Two tiny lines appeared between his brows.

'Sometimes we only find out what we're capable of when we're tested.'

'Well, I think I've failed this test. Maybe I'll do better next time.'

'No.' Immediate and fervent. 'No next times. You don't get this kind of luck twice.'

'Luck?' Was he crazy?

His face grew serious. He glanced at his watch. 'You'll see in a couple of hours. But I'll be right here with you.'

A couple of hours felt like for ever. 'Will the… what do you call it…getting me out…?'

'Extraction.'

'Will the extraction start as soon as the sun comes up?'

'As soon as the sun crests the mountaintops, and assuming there's no fog, yes.'

'How long will it take?'

'Hard to know. We have to stabilise your leg properly and make sure your shoulder is back in its socket before we shift you.'

She swallowed. Both those things sounded very unpleasant.

'And then we'll be pulling you out the back of the car.'

Her face must have paled, because he leaned forward and took her hand. 'I'll be with you every step of the way, Aimee. We'll be tethered to each other at all times.'

'The whole way?'

'Until the top. Until the ambulance.'

She frowned at the finality of that statement. 'Then what?'

He frowned. 'Then that's it. You go to hospital, then home where you belong.'

What if she didn't belong anywhere? And why did she suddenly have the urge never to leave this shattered vehicle and the foil blanket and Sam's gentle touch. 'That's it? I won't see you again?'

He stared at her long and hard. 'I'll see how I go. Maybe I'll drop your luggage back to you when the car's towed up. You'll have plenty to keep you busy before then.'

It was utterly insane how anxious she felt at the thought of that. A man she'd known less than a day. 'I'd like to speak to you again. Under less extraordinary circumstances.' *When I'm showered and groomed and looking pretty.* 'To thank you.'

He nodded even more cautiously. 'I'll see how we go.'

That sounded very much like Wayne's kind of *I'll see.* Her father's kind.

Translation: *no.*

CHAPTER FOUR

'How many siblings do you have in total?' Aimee asked after a while, when her inexplicable and irrational umbrage at his apparent brush off had subsided sufficiently. It wouldn't hurt her to remember that this was business to Sam, no matter how chatty they got waiting for the sun to rise. Maybe rapport development was a whole semester unit over at Search and Rescue School. And maybe the two of them just had more rapport than most.

But it didn't mean he'd want to take his work home with him—even metaphorically.

It just meant he was good at his job.

'Seven,' he murmured, leaning forward and blowing hot air into the cupped circle of her hand, still inside his. He pressed his lips against her fingertips for a tantalising, accidental moment. They were as soft and full as they looked. But warmer. And the sensation branded itself inside her sad, deluded mind.

Wayne had kissed her fingers many a time—and lots of other places besides—but while his lips had felt pleasant, even lovely at the beginning, they'd never snared her focus and dragged it by the throat the way the slightest touch from Sam did. She'd even started to wonder whether she was physically capable of a teeth-gnashing level of arousal, or whether 'lovely' was going to be her life-long personal best.

Please don't let this be the drugs talking. Please. She wanted to think she was capable of a gut-curling attraction at least once in her life.

'I'd definitely want more than one child,' she said, then snapped herself to more attention when she heard her own dreamy tone. 'Speaking as an only child, I mean. I'd want more.'

'Your parents never did?'

'Mum did, I think.' But Lisbet Leigh hadn't been the pants-wearer in their family. 'Dad was content with just me.'

'Why *"just"* you? I'm sure they are very proud of their only daughter.'

She let her head loll sideways on its neck brace. His way. 'You really are an idealist, aren't you?'

Was his total lack of offence at her ant-induced candour symbolic of his easygoing nature or of something more? Was Sam as engaged in her company as she was in his? Or was she just chasing rainbows? Maybe even painting them?

'I'm sure my father will be eternally disappointed that his one-and-only progeny wasn't really up to par,' she continued.

'Define par.'

She shrugged, and snuggled in tighter into her foil blanket. 'You know… Grades. Sports. Achievements.'

'You work for the country's leading science and culture body. That's quite an achievement.'

'Right. And I had good grades. Not record-breaking, but steady.'

'I can imagine.' He smiled, and it reminded her a little bit of the way people smiled at precocious children. Or drunks. She didn't like it.

'You're humouring me.'

'I'm—'

Choosing your words very carefully…?

'—just enjoying you.' He almost fell over himself to correct himself. 'Your company. Talking.'

Well… *Awkward, much?* 'Anyway, nothing short of medicine or law was ever going to satisfy my father. He's had high expectations of me my whole life.' And was constantly disappointed. Ironic, really, when she considered how his marriage had ended. Imploded. And how little he'd done to save it.

'Do you like what you do?'

'I *love* what I do.'

'Then that's what you're meant to be doing. Don't doubt yourself.'

His absolute certainty struck her. 'What if I might love being a doctor, too?'

He shrugged. 'Then that was where you'd have found yourself. Life has a way of working out.'

His assured belief was as foreign to her as it was exhausting. How would it feel to be that sure—about everything? She settled back against the seat and let her eyes flutter closed for a moment, just to take the sting of dryness out of them.

'Aimee—'

Sam was right there, gently rousing her with a feather touch to her cheek.

'I can't even rest my eyes?'

'You went to sleep.'

Oh. 'I can't sleep?'

He stroked her hair again. Almost like an apology. 'When you get to the hospital you can sleep all you want. But I need you to stay awake now. With me. Can you do that?'

Stay with me. Her sigh was more of a flutter deep in her chest. 'I can do that.' But it was going to be a challenge. It had to be four a.m. and she'd left at six yesterday morning. Twenty-four hours was a long haul, even if she *had* had some unconscious moments before he'd found her. And apparently another just now.

'Tell me about your research,' he said, clearly determined to keep her awake. 'What's your favourite story?'

She told him. All about wrinkled, weathered, ninety-five-year-old Dorothy Kenworthy, who'd come to Australia to marry a man she barely knew eight decades before. To start a life in a town she'd never heard of. A town full of prospects and gold and potential. About how poor they'd been, and how Dorothy's husband had pulled a small cart with his culture-shocked bride and her belongings the six-hundred kilometres inland from the coast to the mining town he'd called home. How long love had been in coming for them; about the day that it finally had. And about how severely Dorothy's heart had fractured the day, seventy years later, she'd lost him.

Stories of that kind of hardship were almost impossible to imagine now—how people had endured them—overcome them—and were always her favourites.

'Dorothy reminds me that there is always hope. No matter how dire things get.'

Sam's brow folded and he drifted away from her again. Not because he was bored—his intense focus while she'd been telling the start of the story told her that—but because he'd taken her words deep inside himself and was processing them.

'Why didn't she give up?' he eventually asked. 'When she was frightened and heatstroked and feeling so…alien.'

'Because she'd come so far. Literally and figuratively. And she knew how important she was to her husband. She didn't want to let him down.' His frown trebled as she watched. 'Plus she'd made a commitment. And she was a woman of great personal honour.'

'Is that something you believe in? Honouring commitments?'

'What do we have if not our honour?'

Finally his eyes came back to her. 'Is it her story on your thumb drive?'

'No. It's another one…'

She told him that one too. Then another, and another, sipping occasionally at the water he meted out sparingly and not minding when he shared from the same bottle. She didn't care if Search and Rescue Sam gave her a few boy germs while he was giving her the greatest gift any man in her life had ever given her.

He listened.

He showed interest. He asked questions. He didn't just listen waiting for an opportunity to talk about himself, or slowly veer the subject around to something of more interest to him. He *heard* her. He didn't interrupt. And he wasn't the slightest bit bored.

Just like that a light came on, bright and blazing and impossible to ignore, right at the back of Aimee's mind.

That was the kind of man she wanted for herself. That was the kind of man she'd never really believed existed. Yet here one sat: living, breathing evidence—her already compromised chest tightened—and the universe had handed him to *her*.

How had she ever thought a man like Wayne was even close to worthy? Maybe if she'd been allowed out more as a young girl, had got to meet more people, sample more personalities…Maybe then she never would have accepted Wayne's domination of her. Maybe if she hadn't grown up watching it, until her father had finally forced her mother's hand…

'I can see you love these stories.' His blue eyes were locked on her so firmly, but were conflicted, yet immobile. 'You're…glowing.'

Unaccustomed to the intensity he was beaming at her, and still unsettled by her thoughts of just a moment before, Aimee took shelter in flippancy. 'Maybe it's the glow-sticks.' She smiled and settled against the seat-back, her body begging her to let it drift into exhausted slumber. 'Or the sunrise.'

That seemed to snap him out of his blue-eyed trance. Around them the light had changed from the total absence of any light at all during the night to a deep, dark purple, then a navy. And the navy was lightening up in patches by the moment.

Sam glanced at his watch. A dozen worry lines formed on his face. 'Okay Aimee, the darkness is lifting. We made it.' He found her hand and held it. 'I'm going to need you to be very brave now, and to trust me more than ever.'

We will not fall. She heard the words though she knew he didn't say them.

It only took another few minutes before she realised why a new kind of tension radiated from his big body and from the hand he'd wrapped so securely around hers. The deep blue outside seemed to dilute as she watched it, and darkness began to take on the indistinct blurs of shape. Then they firmed up into more defined forms— the tree branch outside the window, the hint of a hill on the horizon—as the first touch of lightness streaked high across the sky.

Her heart-rate accelerated as it struggled to pump blood that seemed to thicken and grow sluggish.

Around them she saw nothing but emerging treetops—some higher than her poor battered Honda, some lower. The front of the car was in darkness longer than the areas around it because the nose was buried in a treetop. Literally balancing in the crown of a big eucalypt, which threw off its distinctive scent as the overnight frost evaporated. In her shattered side mirror she could see the angle of the hillside—steep and severe— that the back of her little hatchback had wedged against.

And they perched perilously between the two, staring down into the abyss.

A black dread surged from deep inside Aimee's terrified body. She sucked in a breath to cry out but it froze, tortured, in her lungs and only a pained squeak issued, as high as the elated morning chorus of the birds around them but infinitely more horrified.

'Hold on to me, Aimee….'

Sam's voice was as much a tether as any of the cables strapping her into her car, and she clung to it emotionally even though she couldn't rip her eyes from the scene she hung suspended over, emerging through the shattered windscreen, as the sun threw clarity across the morning and finally lifted the veil of darkness.

Her squeak evolved into a primitive whine and her entire body hardened into terrified rigour. The shadowy blur of Australian bush below them resolved itself into layer upon layer of towering treetops, falling away for hundreds of meters and narrowing to a sliver of water at the bottom of the massive gully she'd flown over the edge of.

Half a kilometre of deathly fall below the tenuous roost of her car, wedged between the treetop and the mountain.

Sam! Sam!

She couldn't even make vowels, let alone call to him. The only movement her body would allow was the microscopic muscular changes that pushed air out of her body in a string of agonised whimpers. Like a dog with a mortal injury.

'Look at me, Aimee...'

Impossible... It was so, *so* much worse than she'd feared even in her darkest moments. *Luck,* he'd called it, but it was more of a miracle that her car had hit the crown of this tree rather than plummeting straight past it and down to the tumbling rapids at the bottom of the gully. She'd have been dead before even getting down there, ricocheting off ancient trees like a pinball. Every single base instinct kept her eyes locked on the source of the sudden danger. The threat of the drop. Horrible, yet she couldn't look away.

Her heart slammed so hard against her ribs she thought they might crack further.

Sam forced himself into her line of vision, stretching across her to break the traction of her gaze on the certain death below. The shaft of pain from the extra pressure on her leg was more effective than anything in impacting on her crippled senses.

'Aimee…!'

Her eyes tried to drift past him, her face turning slightly, but he forced her focus back to him with insistent fingers on her chin.

'At me, Aimee… Look only at me.'

Only at me. She heard the words but couldn't process them. This was like last night all over again. *It's the shock,* something deep down inside her tossed up. It was the shock preventing her from looking at him. Understanding him.

The whining went on, completely independent of her will.

Sam slid both warm hands up on either side of her face and forced it to him. This close, he all but obliterated the dreadful view down to the forest floor. In that moment her whole world became the blue of his eyes, the golden tan of his skin and the blush of his lips.

'Aimee…' Sam's voice buzzed at her. 'Think about Dorothy. Think how frightened and alone she felt out there in the desert—fifteen years old, with a man she'd only just met. Think about the courage she would have had to have to go with him. To get onto that boat in Liverpool and leave her entire family for a hot, hostile country. Think about how hard she would have fought against the fear.'

The most genteel, gentle woman she'd ever

interviewed. And the toughest. Words finally scraped past her restricted larynx. 'She had her husband…'

'You have me.' He ducked his head to recapture her eyes. 'Aimee, you have me, and I'm going to get you out of here.'

This time her eyes didn't slide away, back to the void below them. They gripped onto Sam's.

He sighed his relief. 'There you are. Good girl.' He leaned in and pressed his hot lips to her clammy forehead.

The reassuring intimacy just about broke her again. 'Sam…'

'I know.' He dropped back into his position, lying across her, between her and the awful view. 'But you're okay. Nothing's going to happen to you. Not while I'm around.'

She blew three short puffs through frigid lips. 'Okay.'

Sudden noises outside drew his focus briefly away, and when it returned it was intent. 'Aimee… The extraction team are getting into position. Someone else is going to be taking over, but I'm not going to leave you, okay? I want you to remember that. We're going to get buffeted and separated for moments, but I'll always be there. I'm still tethered to you. Okay?'

She nodded, jerky and fast, curling her hand hard around his, not wanting to let go. Ever.

He stroked her hair back. 'It's about to get really, really busy, and no one's going to ask your permission for anything. They'll just take over.

You're going to hate that, but be patient. You'll be up top in no time and then you're back in charge.'

Her laugh was brittle and weak at the same time. 'I thought *you* were in charge.'

His smile eclipsed the sunrise. 'Nah. You just let me think that.'

She sobbed then, and pulled his hand to her lips and pressed them there. He rested his forehead on hers for a moment as the clanking outside drew closer.

'I wet myself,' she whispered, tiny and ashamed.

He wiped a tear away with his thumb. 'It doesn't matter.'

'I don't think I can do this.'

'You can do anything in this world that you set your mind to, Aimee Leigh.'

His confidence was so genuine, and so awfully misplaced, but it filled her with a blazing sort of optimism. Just enough to get her through this.

Just enough to do something really, really stupid.

She stretched as far forward as the flexi-straps would allow, pulled him by his rescue jacket towards her, and mashed her lips into his. Heat burst through her sensory system. His mouth was just as warm and soft as it had felt on her fingers, but sweet and strong and surprised at the same time, and salty from her own tears. She moved her lips against his, firming up the kiss, making it count, ignoring the fact that he wasn't reciprocating. Just insanely grateful for the fact that he hadn't pulled back.

Her heart beat out its triumph.

An unfamiliar face dropped in spider-like at their side window just as Sam tore his mouth away from hers. A dozen different expressions chased across his rugged features in a heartbeat: pity, embarrassment, confusion, and—*there!*— the tiny golden glow of reciprocal desire.

The man suspended in space outside the car did as good a job of schooling his surprise as Sam did—maybe they were all trained to mask their feelings—and immediately cracked the glass of her driver's side window. One part of her screamed at the intrusion of sudden noise and calamity, but it was just as well.

What would she have said otherwise?

Sam gathered himself together faster. He looked out at the crew now swarming over the Honda and then back at her. And then he smiled. In that smile was understanding, forgiveness, and just a trace of regret.

He brushed her hair back from her face again, and Aimee thought she'd never be able to brush her own hair without imagining his callused fingers doing it for her.

'Okay, Aimee,' he said. 'Here we go.'

And as a second man scrabbled into the back of the hatch and squeezed himself around the tree limb still buried there Sam smiled and winked at her.

'Race you to the top.'

It took nearly three hours for the emergency crew to cut Aimee free, get her safely fixed onto a spine board, and carefully slide her backwards out of her car and up the gully-face to the waiting ambulance.

Sam hadn't been kidding about his crew taking over. She was pushed, pulled, yanked and poked every which way, and only Sam was there to dose her up with ant juice and look out for her dignity, tied to her the whole time by his industrial umbilical cord. But she stayed silent and let them do what they had to do, and closed her eyes for the entire last third of it, because watching her own ascent up the hillside required more strength than she thought she had. She tuned her mind in to the sound of Sam's voice—capable and professional as he gave instructions and followed others.

'Last bit, Aimee,' he said, close and private, as they finally pulled her up onto the road she'd gone flying off. 'It's going to get even more crazy now.'

She turned her head towards him as best she could in her moulded spinal brace and opened her mouth to thank him, but as she did so someone stuck a thermometer into it and she found herself suddenly cranked up onto wheels and rushing towards a waiting ambulance. He jogged alongside like her personal bodyguard, and in the split second before she was surrounded by paramedics she thought how little she would mind being protected by a man if it was a man like Sam doing the protecting.

Yet how ironic that she'd practically run away

from the first two phases of her life because she'd been smothered.

She lifted the pained fingers of her dislocated arm in a limp kind of thank-you, but he saw it, jogging to a halt as they reached the ambulance. He unclipped his tether.

'Goodbye. Good luck with your recovery.' He was one hundred percent professional in the company of his peers, and her stomach dropped. Had she truly imagined the closeness between them?

But then she caught the expression in his eyes—wistful, pained—and he lifted a damp strand of hair from her face, those lips she'd pressed her own against whispering silently, 'Live your life, Aimee.'

And then he was gone, and she was strapped unceremoniously into the back of a clean, safe ambulance, mercifully sitting on four wheels up on terra firma. She craned her neck as much as her tight restraints would allow and tried to track Sam in the suddenly chaotic crowd.

Emergency crew. Farmers with heavy loaders. Onlookers milling around. Presumably all the people who couldn't get along the A10 because her rescue was in the way.

But then there he was—straightening out his kinked back and reaching for the sky with the fingers that had first stretched out to her in the darkness. Even with his heavy rescue gear on she knew that his body would be hard and fit and healthy below it.

An irritating orange blur blocked her view,

and she tried to look around the emergency crew member who had climbed into the ambulance after her.

'Sam said you needed this,' the stranger said, placing her handbag on the gurney next to her.

Aimee's eyes fell on it as though it was a foreign object.

'It is yours?' the man asked, suddenly uncertain.

Aimee made herself remember that this man had spent a freezing night on a mountain to save her life, and that it wasn't his fault Sam had reneged on his promise to bring it to her in the hospital.

'Y-yes. Thank you.'

Sam knew how much she was worried about the oral history on the thumb drive inside. He didn't want her separated from it for longer than necessary. Her eyes drifted back to him again as the stranger shifted slightly in the ambulance and her heart swelled.

Such a good man.

But, as she watched, a fragile, porcelain-featured woman hurried through the throng of onlookers and hurled herself at Sam—*her* Search-and-Rescue-Sam—and threw slim arms around his neck. Those masculine arms that had kept her so safe on the hillside slid automatically around the woman's waist and he picked her up, swinging her gently around as she buried her face into his neck.

The orange blur blocked her view again as the stranger turned to climb out of the ambulance.

'Wait! Please!' Aimee called out to him, and he turned back. 'That woman…with Sam. Who is she?'

It never occurred to her not to ask, and it clearly never occurred to him not to answer, because he turned around, located them in the crowd, and then brought his gaze back to Aimee.

'Oh, that's Melissa,' he said, as if that explained it all. 'Sam's wife.'

CHAPTER FIVE

Eleven months later

Wow. Where had the year gone?

Sam caught the sideways glance of the woman next to him and pressed a damp palm onto his right thigh to still its irritating bounce. He straightened, then shifted, then loosened and re-fixed his tie one more time. What he wouldn't give to be hanging off the side of a mountain somewhere, rather than sitting here today…waiting. To either side of him was a mix of old and young, male and female, trained professionals and passers-by. All nervous—like him. All lined up—like him—to get their handshake from the Governor General and a commendation for bravery.

A commendation for doing what he was paid to do.

He shook his head.

He'd participated in six other rescues in the eleven months since he'd hauled Aimee Leigh's battered car up that cliff-face. Since the ambulance doors had slammed shut on that rescue and raced off down the winding A10. No sirens. The best news in an otherwise crappy day. No sirens meant no critical emergency. No sirens meant his assessment of her injuries and his handling of them as they'd carefully winched Aimee up the rock-face had been correct. Busted leg, dislocated shoulder, chest bruising.

No sirens meant the tree had come off worse than she did.

Thank God.

Her little car had been a write-off. She'd been fond of it, judging by the gloss in its paint work and the careful condition of its interior before nature tore it to pieces, and he'd become pretty fond of it, too, by the time they'd finished examining the towed up wreck. How something that small had managed to preserve the precious life in it against an impact like that...

Pretty miraculous.

'Gregory?' a voice called down from the top of a small set of temporary steps. 'Sam Gregory?'

Damn. His turn.

For lack of any other kind of moral support here today he turned to the stranger next to him and lifted his eyebrows in question. The older woman gave him a quick visual once over and a reassuring nod, then wished him luck as he pushed to his feet, tugging at the suit that felt so foreign on him.

But Mel had nagged him into wearing it.

Not that she'd know if he'd switched out of it

halfway to the ceremony today, as he'd used to when he ditched school. Maybe he could have skipped the whole thing—gone sightseeing in Canberra instead. She'd have no idea.

She wasn't here.

She'd said she would come, but she'd been gnawing her lip at the time, and he knew she had a lot going on at work. Knew she'd be here under sufferance. And that was worse than having no one here.

Or so he'd thought at the time.

'This way Mr Gregory,' the assistant stage manager murmured, walking with him to the edge of the enormous drapes which framed the simple setting on stage. The recipient before him was standing awkwardly in the centre of the stage as the master of ceremonies segued into amateur mobile phone video of a man—the awkward man—dangling by braced legs off the edge of a bridge in the north of their country, snatching survivors from torrential flood waters as they tumbled under it. He'd caught and saved three people that day. No one was talking about those that his numb fingers hadn't been able to hold on to.

That's heroic. A man who'd been servicing a farm truck one minute and was risking his life for strangers the next. No training. No equipment. No crew backing him up. No time to change his mind. The only man left standing as an inland tsunami careened through his town.

Sam flexed his shoulders. Why anyone

thought *he* was worthy of even standing on the same stage as a guy like that…

He'd wanted to knock it back when his supervisor had first told him of the nomination. But his boss had guilted him into coming, warning him that not accepting it with grace was an insult to the men and women he worked with who'd missed out on being nominated.

'Do it for the Unit,' Brian had urged.

So here he was, dressed up in a monkey suit, taking one—quite literally—for the team, walking onstage right after a bona-fide hero to accept an award for just doing his job.

The man by his side signalled to his equivalent on the opposite corner of the stage as the video finished and the lights rose, and Sam's eyes followed across the open space. There were two people over there, the second one mostly in shadow because of the bright stage lights between them, but Sam knew instantly who it would be. His chest tightened.

Aimee.

The other reason he'd come. She was here to hand him his award. He needed to look at Aimee Leigh and know that she'd made it—know his efforts had not been in vain and that she'd gone back to a normal, healthy, *long* life.

He needed closure.

Maybe then she'd quit stalking his dreams.

'Stand by, Mr Gregory…'

A low murmur next to him. The live point in his throat pulsed hard enough to feel.

The MC finished his speech and the farmer on stage stepped forward—every bit as awkward and uncomfortable in *his* brand-new suit as Sam was—and accepted the glinting medal offered to him by the immaculately dressed Governor General.

It hit Sam then what a big deal this was, and how right his boss had been. This gong was for every single one of his colleagues who put their life on the line for others. It really wasn't about him.

Applause—thundering applause—as the Queenslander left the stage, and then the MC glanced their way to make sure they were ready. Then he spoke in dramatic, hushed tones into the microphone. Sam took a deep breath and expelled it in a long, slow, controlled stream.

'Our next recipient spent a long, dangerous night on a cliff-face squeezed into a teetering, crushed hatchback to make sure its driver was lifted to safety...'

Jeez. Did they have to over-sell it quite that much? There had been no teetering, and only partial crushing... Sam used the same techniques he used on rock-faces to control his breathing. *In two, out two...* And then suddenly the venue was echoing with more applause and he was being nudged onto the stage.

Nerves stampeded past his eardrums, merging with the drone of the audience. Hundreds of faces beamed back at him from the stalls, all of them there for someone else's award but perfectly willing to celebrate anyone receiving a commendation that day. The MC was still speaking—going through Sam's service record—but he wasn't really listening. His eyes briefly lifted as the dignitary stepped forward to shake his hand, and he did his best to look sincere through his nerves.

'Thank you, Governor General,' he murmured.

But then his eyes slid of their own accord to the curtain on the far side of stage. The shadow had stepped out into the half-light beyond the spotlight and stood quietly waiting. Perfectly upright. All limbs accounted for.

He sucked in a deep breath. *Here we go...*

'And here today, to present Sam Gregory with his Commendation for Bravery is the woman whose life he saved on that Tasmanian mountainside—Miss Aimee Leigh.'

A spotlight swung round to where Aimee hovered in the wings, and she stepped forward nervously but with determination. Sam concentrated on breathing through his nose. She wore a long lemon skirt and a feminine white blouse, and a killer pair of strap on heels that gave her a few unnecessary inches. He realised then that he'd never seen her standing up. He'd imagined her smaller, somehow, although her height was completely perfect for the strong, brave woman he'd spent the best part of a night with.

In the worst imaginable way...

Her long hair was gone—cut short. One of the things he remembered so clearly about that night was having to slide his hand under her thick crop of sweat-damp blonde hair to check her pulse, but seeing it now, trimmed back to a chaos of wisps around a naturally made up face… It was perfect. Kind of Tinker Bell.

Very Aimee.

For no good reason he suddenly craved a shot of O_2—maybe it would steady him as he stood there under such intense scrutiny from the crowd in the eternity it seemed to take for Aimee to walk across the stage towards him. She'd been dressed down for her drive into the highlands a year ago, and the only thing on her skin back then had been blood and air-bag dust, so he hadn't expected this…*vision.* Perfectly groomed, carefully made-up.

Beautiful.

And, best of all, one hundred percent alive.

But those glistening rose lips weren't smiling as she stepped closer, and she was working hard to keep her lashes down, avoiding eye-contact with him or anyone. Sam's focus flew to the two tiny fists clenched at either side of her. Something about the defensive body-language made his own muscles bunch up. Was she here under sufferance? Or did she hate public displays as much as he did?

'Aimee has asked to be excused from making a speech,' the MC boomed into the mic, 'but we're thrilled she's here to give this commendation to the man who saved her life last year.'

Her high heels drew to a halt in front of the lectern and her green eyes lifted to the Governor

General, who handed her a medal on an embroidered ribbon. Her smile as she took it from him was weak, but it dissolved completely to nothing as she steeled herself to face him. As if she was facing a firing squad.

His gut clenched. He hadn't expected a brass band, but he'd definitely expected a smile. Or something…

'Aimee…?'

She lifted her eyes and they were wide with caution but otherwise carefully blank. Her tightly pressed lips split into a pained smile for the crowd's benefit and she held trembling fingers forward to present him with the medal. Sam took it from her with his left hand and slid his right into the one she offered him—perfunctorily, as if she could almost not bear to touch his hand, let alone shake it.

What the hell…?

This was a woman whose life he'd saved. A woman he'd spent hours talking with, sharing with. Whose pain he'd stroked away. Who'd kissed him in her gratitude. And she couldn't even bring herself to smile at him now. He frowned.

Screw that.

When she went to pull her hand away he held it longer than was necessary, drawing shocked lagoon-coloured eyes back up to his. He locked onto them, and her lips fell slightly apart at his intensity.

'You cut your hair,' he whispered, for her

benefit only. And for something to say. Then he made himself smile through the gravity of this moment.

As if his banal observation was some kind of ice-pick in the glacier of her resistance the blank *nothing* leached from her eyes, and they flashed briefly with confusion before filling with a bright, glinting relief he virtually basked in. Her tense façade cracked and fell away, leaving only the Aimee he remembered from the A10, and before he knew it she was stretched to her toe-tips and throwing her arms around his already tight shirt collar. Completely on instinct his hands slid around her waist and he held her close, returning her embrace.

The crowd leapt to his feet to cheer.

'I missed you,' she whispered into his ear, as though she'd been waiting a year to tell him that. The warmth of her breath against his skin made it pucker. 'It's so good to see you.'

As he held onto a woman who wasn't his wife in front of two hundred people who weren't his friends, Sam realised what those dreams and memories he'd been suppressing had tried to tell him.

He'd missed her, too.

Even though he'd only known her a few hours he'd missed Aimee for *a year,* and kept her close in his sub-conscious. Never quite on the surface—just out of it. As she'd stood in the shadows of the spotlight just now.

Waiting.

His arms tightened further, swinging her just slightly off her feet and forcing her curves more firmly up against him. His commendation dangled forgotten from his fingers.

After all, *this* was all the reward he needed.

Aimee's heart had still not settled twenty minutes later as the two of them stood talking in a quiet corner backstage. She'd dreaded this for so long—but one look from those baffled, wounded blue eyes had totally washed away her resolve, rewound the past eleven-months-nine-days-and-sixteen-hours and thrown them straight back into the place where two complete strangers could feel so instantly connected.

So… It hadn't gone away.

Had she really believed it would?

'You must have people waiting for you?' Aimee hinted at last, giving him a graceful exit point if he wanted one. Just in case she was wrong about the connection.

He shook his head and let the exit slide. 'Nope. I came up to Canberra alone.'

She only noticed she'd suspended her breath when her chest forced her to exhale. 'Your… family didn't come with you?' God, she was such a coward. But she didn't want to ask. She wanted him to volunteer it openly. Honestly.

To prove he wasn't like her father.

'They're all at home. They wanted to fly up but I refused. Too expensive for all of them. I'll go see them before I head back to Tassie. Take the medal.'

'Oh.' What else could she say? There was only one thing she wanted to know, and she couldn't ask it.

Why wasn't *she* here?

He filled the silence where she should have spoken. 'And the Parks Service couldn't spare anyone because they're covering for me being here.' His eyes shadowed briefly. 'And Mel couldn't get away from work.'

Her heart thumped at both the hollow tone in his voice and the unexpected opening. 'Mel?' she asked, all innocence.

'Melissa. My wife.'

It was barely a pause, but it was there. Aimee glanced down at his left hand. Still bare.

He read her expression and his fingers slid in between the buttons of his dress shirt, fished out a gold wedding band on a chain. 'I wear it around my neck. It's too exposed at work.'

Another one of a dozen deluded scenarios crumbled to dust. Like the one in which Sam and his wife were actually divorced but still good friends. Or the one where the orange-clad volunteer had simply made a mistake all those months ago, confused Sam with someone else. Or the one in which they all changed religion and Sam found himself in need of an additional wife.

Anything that meant he wasn't some kind of sleazoid, disguising his married status.

Aimee sighed. The truth was Sam wasn't

hiding his wedding ring, he was *protecting* it. That good-guy gene at work again. 'I'm sure she was really disappointed not to be able to get here today.'

His eyes shadowed. 'Yes.'

The audience burst into applause for the ninth and final recipient on stage and Aimee felt her opportunity slipping away. The ceremony would be over in minutes and he'd go back to his life. Where she wasn't invited.

'Why didn't you mention you were married?' she blurted, and then winced at her own lack of art.

His leonine brow folded. 'Rescue is a—'

Someone rushed past, calling all the recipients together for a newspaper photograph. Sam's lips pressed together to contain his irritation. Then he flicked his eyes back to hers. They glittered with intensity even in the shadows. 'Aimee, are you in Canberra for the day? Would you like to grab a coffee?'

That couldn't be a good idea. Could it? She glanced at her watch and pretended to consider it.

'I'd just like to talk. To find out how everything went after the rescue.'

The rescue. The reason she was here. Surely it wouldn't be civil to throw his medal at him and then run. The man who'd saved her life. She nodded. 'Sure. I have time.'

His broad smile was ridiculously rewarding.

Those white, even teeth. That hint of a dimple on the right. And it was all too easy to imagine that it was relief lingering at its corners.

'Ten minutes!' he said, and then dashed off for his media call.

He's married, a stern voice whispered.

'It's only coffee,' she muttered under the thrum of the ceremony's closing music out front.

But he's married.

Aimee took a deep, mournful breath. She'd been kidding herself if she'd thought she'd put Sam out of her heart as well as her mind. He was always there somewhere, lingering. Popping up at the most inconvenient times. Just waiting to claw his way back into prominence at the first available opportunity.

Reminding her of the kind of man she still hadn't found.

But *married* was more than a deal-breaker for her. Her family had been torn apart when she was a child, thanks to her father applying a rather too flexible interpretation to his vows. She was not about to start messing with someone else's marriage.

No matter how tempting.

Just coffee, though. To say thank you properly, to apologise for the embarrassing kiss, and to wish Sam well with his life… Coffee was public and harmless and agenda-free. Coffee wasn't like a drink at a bar. Or in a hotel room. Or over breakfast. Coffee was just coffee and a little bit of conversation. And then that would be that.

They could part as friends, instead of strangers.

Life would go back to normal.

CHAPTER SIX

'So you were only in for a few days? Amazing.'

Aimee lowered her skirt down her leg, back over the pin-scars high on her calf that she'd just been showing Sam. The only physical reminder she had of her night on the side of a mountain.

'It's good to be able to talk to you about this,' she said, sipping her latte. 'No one else gets it. They look at my little scars and think that somehow reflects the scale of the accident.'

'You haven't talked about it to anyone?'

'The counsellor at the hospital.' *Though mostly about growing up as a human tug-of-war, as it turned out.* 'My friend Danielle.' *Mostly about you.* 'But I only gave my parents the basics…'

'You mean you played it down.' He smiled.

She thought about hedging, but then laughed. 'Only because they were already so freaked out by a two a.m. phone call from your crew.'

'Have you dealt with it at all?'

'Yes. I've gone over it a hundred different ways. Things I might have done differently, *should* have done differently…' She dropped her eyes away. 'I'm pretty reconciled to having handled it as best I could.'

'You were brilliant. You made it so easy for me to help you.'

She lifted her eyes. 'I wanted to thank you. Right after…But you were—' *kissing your wife* '—busy.' She sighed. 'The nomination was the closest I could get.'

'*You* made the nomination?'

She nodded. 'I felt like an idiot. All I knew was the date and location of the accident and your first name. But they did the rest.'

'That changes everything.'

'What everything?'

'I didn't want the award. I thought it was crazy that the state would nominate me for just doing my job. But you…' His eyes warmed the whole front corner of the café and his smile soaked into her. 'You I'll accept it from.'

'Good. You'll never know the difference that day made for me.'

'Tell me now.'

Her eyes flew wide as she lifted them. 'Now?'

'You didn't make a speech at the awards. Make one now. Tell me what it meant to you.'

Words wouldn't come. She opened her mouth to say something pithy, but that wouldn't come either. She shuddered in a deep breath and began at the one place she knew she'd already taken him.

'That night changed me, Sam. You showed me that there was a difference between taking *charge* and taking *over*. I hadn't ever seen that before.'

Three little creases appeared between his brows.

Okay. She wasn't explaining this at all well. She leaned forward. 'It took me a long time to realise that the crash mats my parents surrounded me with as I was growing up was more about them than me. But by then I'd bought into all that care and concern and I'd forgotten how to be independent. Maybe I never even learned.'

Sam frowned at her and waited silently for her to continue.

'Then I met Wayne, and I let him drive our relationship because I'd become so accustomed to other people doing my thinking for me. Taking over. Giving me instructions.'

Sam frowned. 'Like I did.'

She shook her head. 'You showed me that the best kind of capability doesn't come from bossing. It comes from influencing.'

Sam frowned at her again.

'You did it the entire time we were in the car. You wanted me to do things but you didn't order me to. You simply gave me the facts and the reason for your request and your preference and you let me decide. Or you asked. And if I said no you respected that—even when it was the wrong decision. Then you just compensated for my glaring bad calls.'

He looked supremely uncomfortable with the

praise. 'Aimee, I just treated you the way I'd want to be treated in the same situation.'

'Which is how?'

He thought about that. 'Like an adult. With all the facts.' Then his expression cleared. 'Like a team.'

'Yes! I have never in my life felt like I belonged to a team, where we worked together for a solution. It was always about compliance or conflict.' She held up her two hands as though they were scales, with one or other of those words weighing heavily in them.

'Well, I'm glad. We were a team that night. We had equal stakes the moment I climbed into that car, so we deserved equal say on what went down.'

She leaned forward earnestly. 'See—that's a novelty to me. The whole idea of equity. I love it.'

He seemed enchanted by her excitement. But a little bemused. 'I'm glad.'

His gentle teasing warmed her every bit now as it had back in the car. 'Don't laugh at me. This is revolutionary. I don't ever want to go back to being that person who needed permission to get through the day. I still shake my head that I let it happen at all. You saved so much more than my physical self on the mountain.'

'Don't go canonising me just yet. I'm sure you were already halfway to this realisation yourself.'

'What do you mean?'

'You were heading up to the highlands to reassess your life. You'd broken off your dud relationship. You were managing your parents.'

If by 'managing' he meant avoiding... 'Okay, so I wasn't starting from zero, but it took that accident to really spotlight what was wrong with my life. And you were wielding that spotlight.'

He grinned. 'Nice analogy.'

'Thank you. It's the storyteller in me.' She finished her coffee and signalled for another before turning back to Sam, her biggest and most exciting secret teetering on her tongue. 'Anyway, that's why I'm so grateful. It's changed the way I do my work, too.'

He cocked his head.

'I got to thinking about what you said—about how my oral histories collect dust once I'm finished with them.'

Sam winced. 'Aimee, I'm sorry. I probably said a lot of careless stuff that night. I was just trying to keep you awake.'

'You were absolutely right. But I'd been too uncertain of myself before to do anything to change that.'

'Before?'

'That's how I've come to think of things. Before the accident and after the accident.' Actually it was before-Sam and after-Sam, but she wasn't about to tell him that. He'd bolt from the café before his spoon even hit the floor. She pressed her hands to the table, leaned forward, lowered her voice. 'I'm going to write a book.'

His eyebrows shot up. 'Really?'

'Really. I'm going to pull together all the stories I've collected about people who grabbed their futures by the throat and took a crazy chance. People like Dorothy. And how that paid off…or didn't. But the important thing is that they were the navigators of their own destiny one way or another. Oh! That could be the title… *Navigators!*'

He stared at her, bright interest in his eyes as her brain galloped ahead. 'Good for you, Aimee.'

Her lungs struggled to reinflate as the full impact of all that focus hit her. She pushed them to co-operate, and it was almost harder speaking now than back in her squished Honda. 'And it's not because you made me feel like what I do isn't complete… It's because it's *not* complete. These particular stories always resonated for me. I just never recognised it.'

Sam smiled. 'I love the idea, Aimee. Let me know if there's anything I can do to help.'

She straightened, took a deep breath and held his eyes. 'Let me do *you*.'

His whole body jerked back.

'Your story!' she rushed on. 'Oh, my God… Let me interview you for your story.' Heat surged up her throat and she knew there was nothing she could do to change that. Intense Sam was only half as gorgeous as Sam in a full belly-laugh, but he treated her to one now, as she stumbled out of the awkward moment. 'I want to include some more contemporary stories as well, and you're about the most proficient navigator I've ever met. I'd love to include you.'

'My story's not really all that interesting, Aimee.'

'Everyone's story is interesting, Sam. Just not to them.'

He stared at her. 'You're serious? You want to put me into your book?'

'I want to thank you—' She held up her hand as he went to interrupt. 'In a way more meaningful than just an award nomination or a couple of cups of coffee. You were present at the moment that redefined my life and I want to reflect that importance.' She sat up straighter. 'So, yes, I want the man that saved my life in my book.' Such naked insistence still didn't come naturally to her, but she squashed down her instinctual discomfort.

'Can I think about it?'

She took a fast breath. 'No. You'll refuse if you think about it.'

His smile then warmed her heart. 'Look at you, getting all take-charge.'

Her laugh burbled up into an excited squeak. 'I know!'

'Maybe you know my story already.'

'You're a modest man, Sam. It's part of your charm. I understand that you won't want this story to be some kind of reflection of how important *you* think the work you do is, but I really want it to reflect how important that work is— *was*—to me.' She forced herself to keep her

stare locked on him, even while every cell of
Old Aimee demurred, whispered that her insis-
tence was ungracious. Not feminine. *Scandalous.*
'Please say yes.'

His eyes narrowed. 'What's involved?'

'You'll hate it,' she said without the tiniest
pause. 'It involves more coffee.'

A hint of a twitch in his left eye was the only
clue that he was smiling on the inside. But it was
enough. 'If we're going to have more coffee I
need some food to soak it up,' he said. 'Are you
hungry?'

'Ravenous.'

Suddenly she was. After months of barely
picking at even the most delectable meals. Sam
was going to be in her book. Sam was going to
share a little bit of himself with her.

And an entire afternoon.

All of a sudden her chest didn't feel large
enough for the organs in it as she squeezed out
speech. 'What time's your flight?'

He stared at her, his eyes carefully neutral.
'Late enough.'

It was beyond refreshing to see a woman inhale
her lunch the way Aimee did, despite their plates
being piled high with home-cooked Italian food
and herbed bread. He was so used to Melissa and
her friends either fussing about the dressing on
the tiny salad they were expecting their bodies
to function on, or getting stuck into something

more substantial and then punishing themselves endlessly for enjoying it.

The kind of unabashed feeding frenzy he was witness to now reminded him of home. Of his family.

They'd taken their meals to a more comfortable booth, and chatted about other rescues he'd worked on in the past year, and about her heritage work, and whether either of them had been in Canberra before, and then, before he'd even looked away from her, a waitress had materialised from nowhere and was clearing their empty plates and bringing more coffee.

'I may never sleep again,' Aimee joked as she blew the steam off her fourth latte.

But there was something about this afternoon: something blindly indulgent that made a bottomless cup of coffee and pasta carb-loading seem as reasonable as his almost gluttonous need for conversation.

Aimee's conversation.

He knew she was intelligent from their hours in the car, but back then she'd been suppressed by pain and medication and—if her epiphany was to be believed—by her own personal demons. But this Aimee had a lightness and an optimism so untrained and raw it was almost captivating. Like a newly emerged butterfly testing out its wings. Definitely engaging. And thoroughly contagious. So much so that by the time she slid a little digital recorder from her handbag into the centre of the cleared table and set it to record he was no longer dreading his decision to help her out.

'You carry that with you everywhere?'

'Yup.'

Her eagerness touched him almost as much as her innocence prickled at his senses. Taunted him. Drew him. 'You really are excited by this book, aren't you?' he said.

Her green eyes sparkled. 'Beyond words. This idea is one hundred percent mine—sink or swim, for better or worse.'

He twitched, but only slightly. Was the mention of marriage vows intentional? A reminder to both of them to keep things professional? If so, it was it was well timed.

'So…' She adjusted the recorder and pointed one end towards him. 'Tell me about your family. You're the oldest of…what was it?…seven?'

'Eight. Second oldest.'

'Big family.'

'Lots of love to go around.'

'That's nice. So no one went wanting?'

He reeled a little. 'Uh…?'

She smiled so serenely it took the edge off his anxiety about where this was going. 'Don't worry—this isn't some kind of exposé. I just want to get to the heart of your background. I like to leap right in. It saves lots of preliminary warm-up.'

Plus, they'd been warming up all afternoon,

technically speaking. 'Okay, uh…no… No one went wanting.'

'How much of that was thanks to big brother Sam?'

He thought about that. 'We all pitched in and looked after each other. Dad worked pretty long hours so Mum needed support.'

'Were you her favourite?'

'There's a loaded question.' He laughed. 'I felt like her favourite, but I'm sure every one of my siblings would say the same. Mum was good like that.'

'Tell me about your parents. How did they meet?'

Sam took her through what he knew of the romance that was his parents' marriage. Some of the challenges, the wins, the losses, their decision to come to Australia and start a new life.

'Sounds almost idyllic.'

'It wasn't without its challenges, but my folks have worked their way through every major bump in their road to happiness. They're great role models.'

'How many of you are married?' she asked.

He blinked. 'Just me and one sister.'

'Too hard to live up to for everyone else?'

His stomach tightened. 'What do you mean?'

'I mean your parents' example. Pretty tough act to follow?'

He struggled against the automatic bristling that came when anyone criticised his family. She was just curious. And she wasn't all that far off the mark, in truth. 'I think we'd all consider it inspirational. Not demoralising.'

She watched him steadily. 'That's nice, then.'

'Yeah, it is.'

'Is that how it is for you?'

His chest matched the tightness in his gut. *Here it comes*. The subject neither of them was mentioning. 'What?'

'Your marriage. Do you aspire to a relationship as strong as your parents'?'

'You're assuming it's not already like that?' And that was a big call on just a few hours' collective acquaintance in which the topic had almost never been raised. He couldn't stop his arms folding across his front.

A hint of colour pinked her cheeks and highlighted the deep green of her eyes. It galled him that his body noticed that even when he was annoyed. He forced his hormones to heel.

'You're right. I am. Sorry. I just…'

But she swallowed back whatever she'd been about to say. So he called her on it: partly to see just how strong her reinforced spinal column really was, and partly because he wanted to see what had made her assume as she had. If he was giving off clues to strangers that his marriage wasn't rock-solid, did that mean Mel might pick up on them, too?

'Just what?'

A dozen expressions chased across her expressive eyes and finally resolved into caution. 'She didn't come. Today,' she added when he just stared at her. 'Today was a really big deal and she didn't come. And I know that the complimentary air tickets were for two because I didn't use my plus-one either.'

She had no one to bring. His antenna started vibrating with a bit too much interest at that piece of information and so he buried it under a landslide of hastily whipped up umbrage and forced his focus where it belonged. Defending Melissa was second nature.

'She works. Hard.'

'I know. You said.' Then Aimee leaned forward and he got a flash of cream curve as her breasts rose and fell. 'But so does your father, and I'm guessing he would have moved the earth to be there if it was your mother shaking the Governor General's hand and being recognised by his country.'

A cold, twisted kind of ugly settled in his belly. It was sixty percent righteousness, forty percent guilt, and one hundred percent reflex. He'd had *exactly* those thoughts himself. 'Are *you* offering me relationship advice? Seriously?'

His subtle emphasis on *you* didn't escape her, and the hurt and disappointment in her expression were immediate. As if she'd been suspending breath, waiting for something to happen.

And he'd just been that something.

Shame bit—down low.

'No.' She smiled, but it was half-hearted and without the luminosity of before. 'That would be like asking me to get *you* out of a stricken vehicle on a mountain. It's just not in my skill set.'

He hated his own overreaction almost as much

as how fast she was to put herself down when challenged. Both smacked of long-standing defensive tools. So her healing was still a work in progress, then.

She went on before he could. 'But I do know something about people. And subtext. I'm trained to read between the lines.'

'My relationship with Melissa is *not* fodder for your book,' he stated flatly.

'You think your wife is not material to your life story?'

He wiped his hands purely for the satisfaction of throwing his serviette down onto the table. The international symbol for *this discussion is over*. 'I think if you want to include her then we should get her agreement.'

This was where a polite person would step back, oil the waters. Aimee just leaned forward. 'You're protective of her.'

'Of course I am. She's my wife.'

'You love her.'

'She's my wife,' he reiterated.

Her perfect face tipped. 'Why are you so defensive?'

'Why are you so pushy? Are you upset I didn't tell you I was married? I met Melissa through one of my brothers, we were together two years and then we got married. End of story.'

Except that was complete bull. There was so much more to their story.

A hint more pink crept into her cheeks. Or was it just that the colour around it had faded? She leaned forward again, lowered her voice. 'Why didn't you mention her to me before? There were so many opportunities.'

A dangerously good question. Was it because he'd felt the simmering *something* between them in their perilous little nest on the mountainside and hadn't wanted it to evaporate? Was he that desperate for a hint of attraction, even back then?

Uncertainty clenched, tight and unfamiliar, in his chest.

'It was none of your business.' Present tense included. *How do you like that subtext?*

Her face froze and her fists curled into nuggets on the table. She took a moment collecting herself. It reminded him of something…

'I…' She pressed her lips together, sat back.

It hit him then—what he was being reminded of. Aimee looked right now as she'd looked back on that mountainside. Pale…stiff. When she'd been in shock, but trying not to let on. It was such a direct echo of how she'd looked all those months ago, hanging off the side of the A10, that he couldn't help the memories surging in. How close he'd felt to her when she was toughing it out in the darkness. How impressed he'd been at her calmness under pressure. How open she'd been with him about her fears and vulnerabilities. How hard he'd worked to keep her safe.

How connected he'd felt to her.

Apparently mutual.

Even now, after he'd just been a bastard and hurt one of the most open and innocent people he knew rather than manning up to his own inadequacies.

It was palpable.

He shifted to dislodge his body's intense focus.

'You know…' Her face twisted in concentration. 'I owe you an apology, Sam. I've spent so much time dwelling on those hours up in the highlands I think I've…' she physically grappled for the right word '…infused them with too much meaning. That day was life-changing for me, but it really was just business as usual for you. No wonder you're uncomfortable with the nomination. With my obsession on having you in my book.' She reached forward and turned off the recorder, her eyes averted. 'I'm so sorry.'

Shame gnawed at his intestines. He was being an ass. 'Aimee…'

She forced her earnest gaze back to his. 'I wanted to do something as meaningful for you as you did for me that day. And I don't have anything to give you other than my interest and the way I see your story fitting into my book. I can't offer you anything else to express how much you did for me.'

'You don't need to.'

'I do need to. For me. I need to…balance the scales.' She reached for her handbag. 'But I've forced a connection that isn't there for you, and I'm sorry.'

Everything inside him twisted. 'Don't leave…'

Her laugh was brittle and her hurried words were for herself. 'I've already made a fool of myself with you once. I really should learn from my mistakes.'

That kiss. So she did remember it. 'Aimee—sit...'

A tiny frown braved the storm of recrimination blustering around it. 'I wish you all the best for the future, Sam.' She was on her feet and swinging her bag onto her shoulder, and then a heartbeat later she was stepping away. Walking away. Doing what he should do. What was best all round.

But he knew he wouldn't. He stood.

'So that's it?' The corner of his lip practically curled. *'Thanks for saving my life, Sam. Have a nice life.'* Two people at nearby tables tried very hard to pretend they hadn't heard that.

Aimee slowly turned back to him, her face guarded. 'You want my firstborn in return?'

Frustration ripped at him. He was screwing this up. Royally. 'Don't leave, Aimee.'

She stood like the proverbial salt pillar, indecision etched into her expression. So he battled on. Risked exposing his true self. 'Your rescue was not business as usual—though it should have been. I don't know what that means, and I don't want to read into it, and I absolutely don't want to *do* anything about it.' He sucked in a breath, and the people at the next table abandoned their efforts to not listen in. 'But you of all people asking me about my marriage was just too...'

He ran out of courage. And words. And air.

Her handbag slipped off her shoulder and she

twisted the strap in her hands. 'Do you want to talk about it?'

'No. Not at all.' But, yes, he really did. Aimee Leigh was the last person he should want to talk about his marriage with, but just then she was also the *only* person he could imagine talking about it with.

'All right.' She collected the handbag in front of her. Its next stop was surely back on her shoulder and swinging out through the door.

Suddenly all his priorities shrank down to just one simple one: keeping Aimee in this café. 'But I don't want us to part like this, either. I'm sorry for snapping. I'm…not used to talking about my personal life.'

She smiled, and it was so full of sorrow she might not have bothered. 'No. I think we should quit while we're ahead. I'll pretend you never answered as you did if you'll pretend I never asked what I did.'

'Make-believe works for you?' He hoped so, if it meant her last memory of him wasn't his being an ass.

The handbag was up and on her shoulder now. 'Let's both agree to try.'

She was turning, and he missed her already. 'What about your book?' It was desperate, but if it kept her here…

She paused, but didn't turn back. She looked at him over her shoulder. 'Maybe another time. Bye, Sam.'

'I'll hold you to that!' he called as she moved decisively through the door.

And then she was gone.

Again.

This time it was his fault.

CHAPTER SEVEN

THE universe wanted her to resolve this, clearly.

If it didn't, it would have left well enough alone and allowed her to just walk out of that café and never see Sam Gregory again outside of her dreams. Now here he was, in the rock-hard flesh, leaning casually on the counter of the airport coffee lounge with his back to her, wearing a light, earthy sweater and sinfully snug jeans.

Her throat tightened just slightly. It had to be a bad thing that she knew him so instantly from behind.

The weeks of separation hadn't done a thing to scrub him from her mind. If anything the passage of time had only exaggerated him in her subconscious. And six days of anticipation since she'd agreed to the State Government's request hadn't helped her to be ready for this moment.

If anything they'd made it worse.

She stopped just a few safe feet from him, suppressed her natural urge to get closer, and took a deep, confident breath. 'Sam.'

Nothing.

She stared at his oblivious back. His broad shoulders shifted just slightly and his right foot tapped on the edge of the counter's kick-bar. She caught a flash of a white wire poking from his ear.

Was he…dancing?

While her stomach ate itself from the inside? Clearly this wasn't as big a deal for him.

She cleared her throat and laid her fingers on his warm bicep to get his attention.

He jerked with surprise, then turned and smiled at her, yanking earphones from his ears. He quieted the tinny *tsss-tsss* with the press of a button in his pocket.

Warm eyes rained down on her and her stomach tumbled in on itself. 'You came. I wasn't convinced you'd actually show up.'

She almost hadn't. Should she be trusted with Sam on an interstate flight? Spending her days in close confines with him? Staying in the same hotel? He hadn't got any worse smelling since she'd last seen him, and the texture of his sweater screamed *touch me*.

She tucked her hands behind her back before she experimented to see if the front of it was as soft as the back. 'Your department was responsible for saving my life and it cost them a lot in equipment and manpower. Coming along on this promotional tour is the least I can do to repay them.'

Even if it put her heart at significant risk.

He took her carry-on bag from her and turned

for the check-in area. 'Apparently we made quite a splash with the public that day in Canberra. My boss's boss wanted this.'

'You didn't?'

He chuckled. 'More time in the spotlight? No, thanks.' Then his eyes found hers. 'But I'm not sorry I get to see you again. I hope to handle myself a bit better this time around.'

Aimee frowned. Straight back into awkward territory. Oh, well, since they were already here... She took a quiet breath and asked as casually as she could, 'Melissa not with you?'

Was it wrong that she wanted him to say yes almost as much as she hoped he'd say no? Having his wife along would solve an awful lot of problems.

'Ah... Three days away from work is more than she could swing. Some imminent breakthrough on an ice shelf project.'

'A what?'

'She works for the Australian Antarctic Division. She's been studying fracture patterns in ice shelves.'

He'd said Melissa was smart. Foolishly, she hadn't believed him. She'd thought it was just what people said about their spouses. 'At least I can bring my work with me. Transcription goes wherever I do.' She looked around anxiously for inspiration. 'So... We'll be talking to schools?'

Talking to schoolkids was another tick in the pro column for coming along: the opportunity to share what she'd discovered about herself during that twenty-four hours on the mountainside. She'd needed quite a few 'pros' to outweigh the big three-lettered 'con' scrawled in the other column.

S.A.M.

'I think so. And some Victorian volunteer groups. Their Parks and Search and Rescue services are separate up there.'

'So this is about more than just publicity?'

'Not for the department, but for me I look forward to the chance to talk to others in the field. Share expertise. Bring something new back to my team.'

'Sounds like we'll be busy.' If there was a God.

'I think there'll be some down time.' His blue eyes seemed to turn luminous.

Oh. *Great.*

Aimee struggled to generate small talk until their flight was ready for boarding. Then getting on the plane and seated and into the air knocked off a good thirty minutes. She busied herself with the in-flight magazine, flicking pages she wasn't reading. It helped keep her from thinking about the way Sam's thigh pressed into hers in the tight seating. And how she was going to survive three days up close with him.

He leaned over the armrest. 'You know, we could probably use this time to get to know each other better.'

If eyes could get whiplash hers would have needed that neck brace he'd once given her.

'What?' she choked, half afraid of the answer.
But only half.

'For your book. We never did finish that interview.'

Oh. 'No. I kind of blew that on my last question.'

His lips twisted. 'What question? I thought we
were forgetting that. Do you have your recorder?'

She slipped it out of her handbag a little too
keenly. When had she started so thoroughly
hiding behind her job? She wanted Sam in her
book, no question, but she could do it without
his wife being in it. Leaping in on his marriage
hadn't been premeditated, but her subconscious
had definitely acted with intent.

Now Sam was buying into her folly. But, as
gift horses went, he was a pretty good-looking
one.

'You're sure about this? I'll need to ask you
about Melissa.'

He took a breath. 'Why don't we start there?
Get it out of the way? I promise not to be reac-
tive.'

A non-reactive man? Another novelty. Assuming he could pull it off. She lowered her food tray,
sat the recorder on it gently and pressed the red
button.

'How old were you when you married?' she
asked over the hum of the jet engines.

'Twenty-one.'

Wow. That made her feel like an old spinster at
twenty-five. 'Young. Is that a Catholic thing?'

'It's a Gregory thing. We don't believe in wasting time.'

His smile was gentle, and she grew aware of how big he was in the cramped seat next to her. Her heart kicked up She shook her head to stay focussed. 'How did you even know who *you* were at twenty-one, let alone each other?'

'I knew. Plus Mel had been a fixture in my family for a long time because of her friendship with my brother.' He studied the digital recorder and didn't quite meet her eyes, making her wonder if there was more to that story.

'How does she feel about the work you do?'

Pained creases appeared above his brow. 'It bothers her. The hours. The disruption to our routine. She's a creature of habit.'

'You being at such risk?'

She'd never seen eyelashes flinch, but Sam's did. 'She doesn't like thinking she could be widowed. The financial uncertainty. I get that.'

The warm glow inside her responded to the misery in his voice. Defending his wife was automatic. Could he hear what he was admitting? Melissa wasn't worried about losing *him,* only her husband, and apparently a large chunk of the household income. 'You never considered giving up the Search and Rescue stuff?'

He lifted his eyes. 'When we have kids. Yes.'

'Which haven't come?'

She knew it was a mistake before the words even left her mouth, but he didn't react. Not the way he had to her suggestion his marriage wasn't solid. This time it was totally unconscious—a deep pain in his eyes. It hurt her to see it. She shifted tangent smoothly.

'You live in Hobart?'

He picked up the new direction gratefully. 'Mel's work has its head office there, so it was a necessary move for her research.'

Necessary. Word choices like that often led her to the true grit in someone's story. If only she had the courage to pursue it. On anyone else she wouldn't have hesitated...But every urge she had to dig into Sam's life suddenly felt loaded and a bit wrong. She hedged instead. 'Quite an achievement, given her young age.'

'She was so excited the day she told me she'd been successfully promoted. It had been a long time since I'd seen her so animated.'

'You were happy to move? Away from your family?'

The look he gave her was pointed. And conflicted. 'We both thought it would be a good idea for us to...start our own lives. Somewhere different.'

'Must have been tough.' And there must have been another reason.

The plane engines were too loud to waste effort with empty words. He just nodded.

'But you had each other. That's something.'

His nod continued, shadows lingering around his gaze. But then they cleared as if by conscious effort. He came fully back to the present. She grew almost uncomfortable under his steady regard as his eyes lifted.

'You're very easy to talk to, Aimee.'

The compliment warmed her and filled her body with helium. But she wasn't about to take it to heart. She couldn't afford to. 'People say that. I guess it's because you have no emotional stake in me. Like talking to a bartender.'

He snorted. 'You don't go to many bars, obviously.'

She wrinkled her nose. 'No, not many. Does that not happen?'

'Not outside of the movies.'

'Oh.'

'Besides, it's not exactly true, Aimee.' Blue heat simmered.

'What's not?'

'We're hardly strangers,' he said. 'We've been through a lot. I...we're friends. Aren't we? No matter how unconventional our meeting was.'

She hesitated to speak, fearing that if she opened her mouth the echo of her hard-hammering heart would come out instead of words. She nodded.

'So it's not true that I have no emotional stake in you at all.'

Her breath caught around the thumping in her chest. What in the world was she supposed to say to that?

'Plus there's...' His hooded gaze was crowded with every thought running through his mind as he deliberated. He reached out and turned off the mini recorder. 'The Kiss.'

Mortified warmth flared through her whole body. Had she really expected the topic to never to come up? She'd spent a lot of time analysing that kiss these past months, reliving it. And though she'd had a hard time regretting giving in to the impulse—even once she knew about the existence of *Mrs* Gregory—she was sorry for the way she'd forced it on him.

But she'd never expected it to earn uppercase status in his mind. *The Kiss*. And she'd really never expected him to raise it so openly.

She struggled for the right words. 'That was my fault, Sam.'

'I wasn't chasing an apology. But I think we need to talk about it. Get it out of the way.'

Really? She just wanted to pretend it had never happened. 'I'm not sure examining it is going to explain it. I was overwhelmed with fear and you were the one keeping me sane. I just needed the…human contact.'

Did she get any points for half-truths? Or did she lose one for the half she was hiding?

'Aimee, you don't need to justify why you did it.'

She frowned. 'Then why raise it?'

He glanced around them at the half-empty plane and then leaned in. 'Because it's stayed with me.'

She stared at him, her breath thinning. Her mental oxygen mask dropped down. 'Stayed?'

'I was on the job. You were hurting. I totally understand why you did it. But what I don't understand…' his blue eyes pierced hers '…is why I let you.'

Her tongue threatened to stick so firmly to her palate that it would be impossible to speak. She was sitting on a plane, heading for a hotel in a different city with a married man she'd non-consensually kissed, taking about said kiss.…

She squirmed. 'I didn't really give you much option—'

'You were tied to your seat. I could have moved out of your reach easily. Why didn't I?' His stare burned into her. 'And why haven't I forgotten it?'

It was hardly going to be uncontrollable lust—for a woman covered in blood and dirt and soaked in her own urine. She stared at him and shook her head: silent, lost.

The chief steward's even tones streamed out of the overhead speakers, advising passengers that they were commencing their descent into Melbourne. She had no idea what he expected. So she did the only appropriate thing.

She brushed it off with a hollow laugh.

'A mystery for the ages!'

His eyes narrowed. 'It doesn't bother you?'

Time to lie! 'It bothers me that I did it. I'm embarrassed, of course.'

'But that's all?'

Time to run! She unclasped her seatbelt. 'I'm just going to…Before we land. I'll be right back.'

But before she'd made it to the next row she heard him behind her. 'We're going to have to talk about it at some point, Aimee.'

She fled. Down the aisle and into the toilet before the seatbelt light came on. She made the most undignified exit of her life from the most excruciating conversation of her life about the most unforgettable kiss of her life.

She slid the 'engaged' knob into place as if it would save her life.

Sam watched the little unisex toilet symbol flick from green to red and he sighed. Pretty appropriate, really. The little man represented him and the little woman represented Aimee. It only took one conversation to push the two of them from an amiable green to a cautionary red.

Red for embarrassment. Red for anger. Red for incendiary.

Take your pick.

The two of them existed perpetually on the edge of an inflammatory zone. His pulse was still pounding. The chemistry between them hadn't eased off since that day at the awards ceremony. He rubbed his thigh where it tingled from pressing against hers. All that unspent tension had to go somewhere.

Even after weeks apart it was still live.

Simmering. Just waiting for an excuse to flare up.

Enough to rattle both of them. Enough that he'd forgotten himself and started a conversation that he'd have been better off not having. So why had he started it? Was he so desperate to forge a connection between them? Or was it because it was the only legitimate way he could relive that moment? The moment on the rock-face when Aimee went from being his patient to something more meaningful.

Something she wasn't asking to be.

Something he couldn't let her be.

But he did enjoy riling her. The colour that flared in her cheeks... The glitter of her eyes... The defiant toss of her hair...

He adjusted his position in the cramped economy seat as his body celebrated the image.

Or maybe he just regressed to being nine years old in her presence and stirring her up was the equivalent of pulling her plaits to get noticed.

Maybe he really was that lame.

Either way, he needed to get a handle on it. They had three intensive days of promotion to get through, and they weren't going to be any easier if he kept teasing her into hiding. They were both adults, and now colleagues. This was officially a work trip. Attraction or not, if he couldn't count on his own best judgement then he'd have to count on his professionalism to get him through.

He glanced at the little red symbol above the bathroom again.

Assuming she ever came out.

CHAPTER EIGHT

AIMEE curled up in the comfy corner of the L-shaped sofa in her hotel suite at the end of their first long day in Melbourne and let her head fall back on a laugh. 'Are you serious?'

'Right in the solar plexus.'

'And she was how old?'

'Eighty-two. She had the bone density of someone two generations younger.'

'Sam Gregory taken out by a great-grandmother.' A frightened, bewildered great-grandmother, who'd had to wrestle with a young bag thief until Sam intervened. 'Can't you go anywhere without rescuing someone?'

'She was doing a great job of holding onto her bag against a pretty big kid. I just evened up the odds for her.'

'And got punched for your trouble.' She laughed again. 'You were supposed to be walking off the craziness of the day. Not hanging out in a police station making a report.'

They'd both run from point to point like mad things since the moment they'd set foot in Tulla-

marine Airport that morning. Two school appear-
ances, then out to a rescue centre at the foothills
to have the same conversations, answer the same
questions. To go over and over the events of that
night on the A10 in excruciating detail.

'Were you scared?' one kid had asked.

'Did it hurt?' This from a young girl.

'Was your car smashed to pieces?' Always a
boy asking that one.

She was so grateful to have him by her side,
but every time Sam told the story he used words
like 'standard operating procedure' and 'proto-
col' and 'training'. Depersonalising the entire
incident. By contrast, her contribution was all
about her feelings, her fears, how much difference Sam's presence and support had made to
her.

Not unlike the whole day, really. And the two
yet to come.

As an exercise in public relations it was text-
book. As a tool to remind her how everyday her
situation had been for Sam—how *not* special—it
was acute.

'I just wanted to explain why I wasn't at
dinner,' he went on.

Reality still haunted her. 'I don't expect you to
babysit me every minute.'

'I know, but this is my city. My turf. I feel bad
that I left you here alone on our first evening.'

Our. As if they were a couple.

'Don't feel bad. I had Room Service soup
and then a long, hot bath. It was blissful.' It had

soaked away some of her exhaustion, but not all. She squirrelled deeper into the sofa and got comfortable on a soft sigh. 'Is that why you called? To apologise?'

There was the slightest of pauses before he cleared his throat and continued. 'Getting fresh air was only part of the reason I went out. Mel turns thirty next weekend and I wanted to pick her up something.'

Aimee smiled past the little twang at the mention of his wife's name. She was going to have to get used to those twangs. 'I'm guessing the inner-city constabulary don't offer a lot in the way of fine giftware?'

Her eyes flew to the adjoining wall as she imagined she heard his rich laugh clean through it. Until that moment Sam being next door to her in the hotel had hovered around her consciousness in a kind of abstract way. Talking by phone, he might as well have been across the country.

But that laugh brought him into pulse-racing context.

Right. Next. Door. Her heart kicked up a beat.

'I have no idea what to get her,' he said.

Really? His own wife? 'None at all?'

'Flowers? Chocolates? Something expensive?'

'Lord, don't use price as your primary parameter...'

'Don't *all* women like expensive gifts?'

Aimee smiled at the genuine bemusement in his voice. 'Not if they're in lieu of intimacy, no. We see right through those.'

'My sister says lingerie, but—'

Her stomach curled. *Oh, God, don't ask me about lingerie for your wife.*

'—won't she think I have an expectation of seeing it on her?'

Despite not wanting to have this conversation, Aimee frowned. 'She's your wife, Sam.'

'Right, but...lingerie's a statement. You know?'

She blinked. What kind of marriage did they have?

Before she could worry that particular bone further he went on. 'In the same way that a toaster is a statement. Or slippers.'

'Do *not* buy her slippers.'

His low, rich chuckle down the line had its usual effect on her. Every hair on her body quivered. 'I won't. Even I know that much.'

She blew out a breath. She owed Sam: bigtime. If gift advice for the wife she wished didn't exist was what he needed, then so be it. She wouldn't fail him. 'Okay, so you want intimate, but not *intimate.*'

'Right. Thank God we have this shorthand, Aimee.'

That made her frown. She stretched on her sofa. 'And you have no thoughts whatsoever?'

'I have heaps of thoughts, but I have no idea which is the best one.'

'Want to throw some at me?'

Pause. Long pause. 'Actually, I was hoping

you might help me out…in person. We have a couple of hours' down-time tomorrow.'

Her spine stiffened again, just as it had started to relax. Being together racing around the suburbs of Melbourne on business she could handle. Being on the other side of a thick hotel wall was doable. Shopping together for a gift for his beautiful, talented wife…?

She got to her feet—all the better to roam around the room.

'Together?'

He laughed again. 'That's the idea. Unless you want to phone in your advice like tech-support?'

Restricting themselves to phone conversations might be the best thing all round. Though she doubted that those few degrees of separation would do much to diminish the way he invaded her thoughts—awake or dreaming—it would at least spare her the confusion and frustration and risk of sitting across a table from a man she couldn't in good conscience touch.

Not in the way her body wanted to.

She stalled him as her mind raced for a way out of this. 'What did you have in mind?'

'The markets?'

Say you're busy. Say you have to work on a transcription. Say you're feeling fluey.

A deep shudder left her in a rush of air. 'Okay.'

She did a shabby kind of rain-dance across the carpeted floor of her suite. *Honestly!* She had the self-determination of a lemming.

When it came to Sam she had absolutely none.

'Fantastic. Thank you, Aimee. I appreciate it.'

Sure he did. Why wouldn't he? She was at his beck and call. And that was a dangerously familiar dynamic. But she pressed her fingers to her temple and took a deep breath. It wasn't Sam's fault she'd reverted to the bad old days. It wasn't his fault the gravel of his voice turned her spine to jelly and her mind to hot, long, imaginary nights.

Not seeing him in person these past weeks hadn't done anything to reduce the *thing* between them. Or the fact that indulging the *thing* wasn't acceptable because of his wife. Because of Aimee's own values.

But she'd committed to helping him—she *wanted* to help him. To do something to even the slate. Though this really wouldn't have been her first choice.

As had become her norm, she took shelter behind her book. 'My price for assistance will be knocking off some more of my interview.'

'The pleasure of my company is not reward enough?'

It couldn't be. She couldn't let it be. She shielded those raw, strained thoughts behind her old friend flippancy. 'You have an unattractively high opinion of yourself, Sam Gregory.'

His smile warmed the earpiece of her phone. 'Looks like my days of trading on your hero-worship are well and truly over.'

Aimee frowned. A lesser man might, in fact, have acted on her sycophantic adoration—wife or no wife. A lesser woman might have let him. But for all he'd tried on the plane to get her to talk about *The Kiss,* Sam hadn't once exploited the complicated emotions she had about the man who'd rescued her. He just wanted to clear the air.

'You'll always be my hero.' That much, at least, she could say. Hand on heart.

'And statements like *that*—' he laughed '—are why I have an unattractively high opinion of myself.'

She grasped the humour he threw out and used it to climb out of the dangerous place they'd just found themselves in. It was safer all round if she didn't go back to those days. Those feelings. 'Just a pity all that talent doesn't stretch to gift selection.'

He groaned. 'Thanks for pointing that out.'

'Well, you know you can always count on me for a healthy reality check.'

'Something to look forward to tomorrow. I'll meet you in the lobby at nine?' he said.

'Make it eight. Something tells me we're going to need all the scouting time we can get.' A loud noise from Sam's end of the phone made her jump. There'd been a lot of rustling, too, as they spoke. 'What are you doing, anyway?'

'Shaving. I'm just out of the shower. That was the bathroom cabinet closing a bit too quickly.'

Her whole body flinched. 'Oh… Okay.'

What exactly was she supposed to say to that?

Her ears grew acutely sensitive to every little sound in the next moments. The way the acoustics changed as he left the bathroom. The pad of his feet on the carpet. The flip of the lid of his suitcase and the rustle of him pulling out some clothes. Pyjamas, presumably.

Heat suffused her.

She turned to the big blank wall that stood as all that separated them. It formed the perfect canvas for her vivid imagination to paint him sauntering barefoot and damp across a suite the mirror image of hers, a fluffy white towel slung low on lean hips, the mobile phone at his ear the only other thing adorning him.

Every bit of saliva in her mouth decamped.

'Well,' she croaked, 'I'll let you go. I have some work to do tonight. See you tomorrow.'

He sighed. 'Yeah, I still need to call Mel. Don't want her to worry.' His voice dropped in timbre. 'See you in the morning, Aimee.'

She practically tripped over her tongue in her haste to end the call, then sat with the phone pressed numbly to her head long after Sam had rung off, her ears tuned, desperately, for any further audio hints from beyond the wall.

Just out of the shower.

While on the phone to her.

She wrestled free of the heated visuals that rushed at her like a line of football players and chewed her lip at a niggling afterthought. Having a conversation with someone while you were naked hinted at a certain kind of intimacy. Husband-wife kind of intimacy. Or oldest mate from childhood.

The latter suggested she'd assumed a genderless kind of role in Sam's mind: totally non-sexual, like a sister or an old friend. The sort of non-wife woman you wouldn't hesitate to have a phone conversation with while wandering around a hotel room in the buff.

Aimee frowned. She didn't want to be genderless with Sam. She didn't want to be his sister. Just because she wasn't actively exercising her femininity on him it didn't mean she wasn't keen to remain feminine in his mind. She liked how sexy she felt when Sam was around. She'd had a lifetime of feeling otherwise. A child…and then a chattel.

But the other possibilities bothered her even more—on a much deeper level. There should only be three women that Sam felt comfortable getting naked with—even telephonically. His mother, his doctor and his wife.

And she was none of those.

Her mind whirled. Did it say something that *she* was the first person he'd called on stepping out of the shower? Or was he just getting her call out of the way before stretching out on that king-sized bed for a longer late-night call with his wife?

That set a whole extra set of visuals flickering past her consciousness, and she shut them down hard.

One way or another Sam's unconscious behaviour was telling her something important about the nature of their relationship. Something that had alarm bells clanging deep in her psyche. Unless she was misreading this through inexperience? Maybe it was a Mars-Venus thing? Maybe guys truly thought nothing of getting naked while they had a woman on the phone, and Sam was just keen to relax after a long and chaotic day?

She let the phone slowly slip down from her ear to rest on her straining breast.

Maybe.

Sam flopped down on the sofa in the corner of his room, folded his arms behind his head and stared at the ceiling.

It couldn't be a good thing that he was still struggling to clear his head of an image of Aimee, all pink and soft from a hot bath, curled up in her complimentary bathrobe with papers spread all around her, working diligently on her transcription. Lifting her head as he walked into her room. Smiling and stretching up for the kiss he would place on her hairline before going back to her work and losing focus on everything but her stories. Leaving him to just…watch her.

Okay, now he was just plain fantasising.

It had been bad enough spending all day together—listening to her soft voice talking to the school kids, vicariously experiencing her fear and anxiety about the accident through the memories she recounted for them, sitting with his body pressed against hers in the compact car that his department had sent to move them around Melbourne. Working so well together as a team.

He really didn't need to add inappropriate fantasies to the many different ways he was *not* helping the situation. Yeah—fantasies in the plural. This wasn't the first that had broken through since she'd walked so cautiously back into his life across that stage all those weeks ago. Since she'd exited the café with such dignity after he'd been a jerk. Since her cheeks had flushed so hot this morning when he'd mentioned the kiss.

The harder he tried to keep Aimee out of his mind, the more often he caught her in there. It was never lewd, never disrespectful. Just flashes of her smile, the smell of her hair, the memory of a touch…

But she wasn't here for his amusement. She was here to help out his department. It wasn't her fault she was also the sweetest, freshest, most distracting person he'd met in…

He sighed.

…a really long time.

His mind made the immediate shift to Melissa. The only other woman that he'd ever obsessed about in quite this way. All the more because he couldn't have her at the time. Four long years of teenage angst and hormone-driven focus until his planets had aligned and he'd had a chance with the girl he'd been secretly admiring for what felt like for ever.

By then he'd built her up to goddess status. The sun had risen and set with her. She was perfection.

How could she ever have lived up to that?

The contrast between the intense attraction he'd felt then, for the girl he couldn't have and the beige, comfortable *nothing* he felt now, just a few years later for the girl he'd eventually married... Had he learned nothing since he was nineteen?

He should know all about heady infatuations.

Was that what he was doing with Aimee? Turning her into some kind of new ideal of the perfect woman for him? Since Melissa had failed to achieve it? Since they'd so miserably failed to achieve perfect couple status together?

Back then, his list of non-negotiables had been a heck of a lot shorter. These days it had become more sophisticated: intelligence, compassion, warmth, someone looking to be stronger in a pair than they were on their own.

His needs had grown beyond the shallow.

They'd certainly outgrown his marriage.

Sam's eyes drifted shut. He should call Mel. Not that she'd asked him to, or would even expect it; she wasn't exactly what you'd call needy. She'd probably be at the lab, working on her ice, not even conscious of the time, enjoying a concentrated opportunity to work without having to worry about getting home to him. She wouldn't appreciate the interruption.

He'd gone to do it earlier—picked up the phone and dialled. But Aimee had answered instead, like some kind of cosmic mistake. He glanced at the last call on the phone still in his hand. Yep. He'd dialled her number without realising.

He'd had to come up with something fast to justify his stuff-up. Mel's birthday was the perfect excuse. Totally real—he'd failed abysmally in getting something for her—but he hadn't started the day planning on asking Aimee for her help finding a gift.

He wasn't that much of a masochist.

He let his head roll to one side on the sofa-back and stared at the wall dividing Aimee's room and his. He pictured her sitting there, all languid and relaxed and sleepy, and his body responded immediately with a torturous tingle. It would take just moments to throw on some clothes, heartbeats to be out in the hall knocking on her door, and fantasy seconds more to get those clothes off again.

As if that was ever going to happen.

He was married.

She was Aimee.

Ne'er the twain shall meet.

He pushed to his feet and dialled Mel's number. It started to ring immediately. Aimee reminded him of the best part of his relationship with his wife. The early golden years when the two of them had still been caught up in a spiral of mutual appreciation and new romance. Back before life had got busy, before they'd both found their feet as adults. Did that place even exist any more? And if it did could he possibly find his way back there? Could *they?*

He shuddered in a sigh.

He'd made Mel some promises that day they'd

stood before a priest and committed to each other for ever, and she'd taken him in good faith.

He owed her as much, too.

The call went to voicemail. His wife's impatient, confident tone suggested even a voice message was an interruption.

His eyes dropped shut and he concentrated on the woman he'd pledged his life and allegiance to, pushing out the one who flirted enticingly at the edges of his mind even when she didn't mean to.

The phone beeped.

'Hey, Mel…' he started.

Hey, Mel…what? Hey Mel, I'm miserable and so are you. Hey, Mel, is it possible we got married for the wrong reasons? Hey, Mel, I'm sorry that I'm not better at loving you.

'I…uh…just wanted to let you know we arrived okay—' *your husband and the woman he can't stop thinking about* '—and that…'

He opened his eyes and stared at the blank wall again. Imagined Aimee there. Wanted to be with her so badly he burned with it. But his loyalty—his life—belonged to someone else.

He had to try harder.

'…just that I'm thinking about you.'

He rang off and dropped the phone onto his bed, then followed it in a defeated kind of body-flop.

He was honouring his wife.

Why did that feel like such a betrayal of himself?

CHAPTER NINE

'No! Definitely no.'

Aimee stood with Sam, deep at the heart of the beachside markets, the historic architecture in pronounced contrast to the modern, brightly coloured pop-up canopies littering the busy square.

Around them, buried beneath a surging crowd of tourists and locals, rows of stalls sold fine oils, organic produce, delicately hewn crafts, original artworks, timber knick-knacks and bright hand-woven beanies. They offered just about every gift imaginable.

But still Sam had found *this*.

He held up a twisted oddity made from forlorn-looking recycled cutlery. 'It's a spoondelabra. You put candles in it.' He blinked at her lack of enthusiasm. 'It's clever.'

Aimeee smiled at the tragedy of his expression and prised it carefully from his fingers. 'No, Sam.'

He frowned and picked it up again as soon as she'd placed it back on the display table. 'I like it.'

Her laugh graduated to a full chuckle. 'Then

buy it for yourself, by all means. You are not buying your wife a *spoondelabra* for her thirtieth birthday.'

She'd taken to calling Melissa *your wife* as a defence mechanism. Not only did it serve as a healthy reminder to her not to get too entangled with Sam, but it helped to depersonalise Melissa, too. As long as she didn't have a name, Aimee felt slightly less guilty about tiptoeing around with someone else's husband on secret business.

Slightly.

A purple-haired woman dressed almost completely in hemp squeezed past them with a small goat trotting happily behind her on a leash. Sam's free hand slipped protectively around behind Aimee as she pressed in closer to him to let the goat pass. She felt his heat and got a whiff of something divine under the wool of his jacket. Definitely not goat. Her eyes drifted shut.

Focus...

'Fine.' He handed the artwork back to its creator with a reluctant smile. The man shrugged and gave it a quick polish before replacing it on the table.

They moved off again through the thick crowds. 'Seriously, Sam. We're not going to get very far today if you buy every little thing that takes your fancy.'

Sam stayed close to her as they walked, shielding her with his body from the worst of the crowd and lowering his head to be heard. 'Who says?

Could work well… If she doesn't like one gift I can whip out another.'

She laughed. 'Right. She'll never notice that.'

'Well, what do *you* like, then? Since *my* ideas apparently suck the big bazoo.'

'It's her thirtieth, Sam. She's not going to want a novelty anything. She'll want something lovely. Something unique. Something that says you know her.'

His lips thinned. 'I *do* know her and I'm still at a loss.'

Yeah? Why was that? She slid her hand around his forearm and squeezed. 'Don't worry, we have a couple of hours yet. We'll find something this morning.'

But his eyes didn't lighten. 'Pretty sure I'm not supposed to need this kind of support team just to buy my wife a gift,' he muttered.

Aimee was feeling sorry enough for herself without him adding his self-pity to the mix. She braced her fists on her hips. 'Well, you can pout about it or you can get on with it. And you've dragged me out of a warm bed on our morning off, so if you're going to pout I might just wander off and do my own thing.'

He stopped and stared as she was towed ahead of him by the crowd. She turned back against the tide and tipped her head in enquiry.

'You reminded me of my mother just then,' he said as he caught up with her.

'Flattering.'

'In a good way. She's very no-nonsense like

that. She wouldn't tolerate self-pity either. I'm not used to that outside of my family.'

Aimee smiled as they set off again, feeling unaccountably light. 'She and I would probably get on well, then.'

'I know you would.'

She detoured physically—and conversationally—stopping in front of a stall with handcrafted silk scarves blowing like medieval banners in the breeze. 'What about one of these? They're beautiful.' The soft fabric blazed rich colour in the mid-morning light.

Sam frowned. 'What will she do with a scarf?'

Aimee blinked. 'Wear it?'

'On her head? Isn't that a bit…nanna-ish?'

She dismissed the concern with a wave. 'Think less *nanna* and more *catwalk*.' She loosened one carefully from its tie point and caressed the cool, soft silk as it slipped through her fingers. 'She can wear it like this…' She looped it quickly around her throat in a fifties kind of knot. 'Or like this…'

She twisted it into different styles to show Sam the many ways Melissa—*his wife,* she corrected herself—could enjoy a beautiful scarf without it being old-fashioned.

'Or if she's really keen she can wear it like this.' She tipped her head forward and twisted the scarf into a hippy headband, pushing it up the line of her shaggy hair. Then she struck an exaggerated catwalk pose and threw Sam a two-fingered peace sign, smiling wide and free.

Blue eyes locked onto hers, entertained and glittering, and Aimee's breath caught at the fire kindling deep in them. The fire she hadn't seen since the careless, unmasked moment after she'd kissed him on the mountainside. Time froze as they looked at each other. But as she watched his smile dissolved, the flames flickered and extinguished, and two tiny lines appeared between his brows.

Her confidence faltered and she let her peace sign drop limply to her side.

'Very Woodstock,' Sam finally said, carefully neutral, but stopped her as she went to slide the scarf off, curling his warm fingers around hers. 'Leave it. Freedom suits you.'

They stood like that—silently, breathless, his fingers coiled around hers—for dangerous moments.

Freedom did suit her. The year since taking charge of her own life had been the best of her whole life. And the hours she spent with Sam the best of those.

'I'll have to buy it,' she murmured.

'Let me.' His wallet was open and the stall holder's hand was outstretched before she could do more than squeak in protest. He finished the transaction: efficient, no-nonsense. Very Sam.

'Thank you,' she said, too unsettled by the gesture to protest. 'Now we *really* need to get Melissa something.' He slid a curious glance her way. She couldn't help her fingers touching the scarf where it curled under her hair. 'It's going to be really dodgy if the only person you buy a gift for today is another woman.' She laughed weakly.

He took his receipt and turned to face her, eyes serious. 'You're not another woman, Aimee. You're you. This is to show my appreciation. For your help today.'

You're you. What did that mean? Not worthy of 'other woman' status, or somehow outside of the definition? Genderless again. 'We already had a deal. I help you with your gift and you help me with the interview. Quid pro quo.'

'Today deserves extra credit.'

A rare, uncomfortable silence fell between them as they stared at each other but then Sam's eyes drifted over her shoulder, flared, and his face filled with animation.

'What about a kite?' he exclaimed, and was off.

'Men really are just little boys in big bodies, aren't they?'

They sat at a weathered timber table beneath a canopy of fragrant flowering jasmine which defied gravity on the pergola over their heads, tucking into an early lunch of cheese, bread, pâté and something peculiar made of eggplant. Aimee dragged her eyes back off the two enormous kites sticking out of a recycled plastic bag and met the mock offence in Sam's with a grin.

'Kites are timeless,' he pointed out. 'Airborne works of art. And good for obesity.'

'I know. I heard the sales pitch too.' Though

she'd never met a man less likely to have issues with obesity now or in the future than Sam. Or more comfortable with his inner nine-year-old. In truth, his passion for life and his willingness to let himself be open in front of her was dangerously appealing. He wasn't endlessly talking himself up, like Wayne, or angling to get anything from her, or making himself look good. He was just being Sam.

And she liked Sam. She really, really did. Just exactly as he was.

More fool her.

She forced a smile to her lips. 'Given you came up trumps for Melissa, I can hardly begrudge you a kite.' He'd bought his wife the most heartbreakingly beautiful mirror, its artisan-made frame inlaid with luminous crystals and with intricately wrought iron vinework twisting through and around the whole piece. *'Symbolic of both of us,'* he'd said when he chose it. *'Melissa's brilliance and my love of nature.'*

Her heart had swollen with pain then—for the poetry in his words, for the sweet uncertain fear he felt about choosing the wrong gift for the woman he was sharing his life with, and for the truth his words revealed about their relationship. Now and again he'd say something that made her think that maybe things weren't all roses at home, but those simple words spoke volumes about his real feelings for his wife. Her heart weighed heavy in her chest.

'Sam, can I—?' Her own judgement stilled her tongue.

'What? Go ahead.'

She frowned at him and thought hard for the moments that ticked by, wondering if she should back out. 'I want to ask you something, but I don't want to offend.'

'I'm having too good a day to take offence.' He slid one big hand on his heart. 'Ask away.'

'It's about Melissa.'

The hand faltered as he lowered it.

'Is everything okay with you two?'

His whole body stiffened up. 'Why do you ask?'

'You're so passionate in your defence of her, so considerate in meeting her needs, so proud and loyal when you speak about her...'

'But?'

She took a deep breath. 'But...your body language and what you're not saying tells a different story.'

His nostrils flared. 'What I'm *not* saying about her tells you more than what I *am* saying?'

'This is what I do for a living, Sam.'

'Are we in the interview now?'

She sucked back her instinctive reaction to the harshness of his voice. 'See—that's very telling to me. That you get so worked up on this particular subject.'

His cheek pulsed high in his jaw. 'Mel and I are fine.'

'Just *fine?* Not great? Not wildly, crazy in

love?' Although she knew the answer to that. If he were he wouldn't have had such a hard time buying her a gift. And he sure as heck wouldn't be sitting here with *her*.

His simmering eyes told her he was trying very hard not to be rude. 'All marriages go through their rough patches.'

She took a breath, trusted her instinct. 'How long has this patch been?'

He dropped his eyes to the table, and when he lifted them they were predatory. 'I think we should talk about that kiss now.'

It was her turn to stiffen. 'Don't change the subject.'

'Don't avoid the subject. Why won't you talk about the kiss?'

She leaned forward. 'Why is it so hard for you to talk about your wife?'

He met her in the middle of the table. 'Same reason it's so hard for you to acknowledge kissing me. It's personal.' He blinked and his voice softened. 'And terrifying.'

She sat back.

Terrifying. Sam Gregory—the man who seemed to be afraid of nothing—was frightened for his marriage. Everything he'd not *quite* said these past days, every 'fine' instead of 'great' came into crashing focus.

This changed everything.

And nothing.

The tightly reined emotion in his eyes said that he was raw and hurting and vulnerable to suggestion; this was not the time to be careless with the knowledge she'd unexpectedly found herself holding. But she could lead by example and have some courage.

'I kissed you before I knew you were married,' she said.

His eyes flared, as if he hadn't truly expected her ever to return to the taboo subject. Maybe he'd thrown it out there as a distraction, but she grabbed it with both hands.

Fair's fair.

'I'm not someone who would ever knowingly...' Her father's wandering eye had wrecked her family. But she couldn't tell Sam that. That wasn't the sort of thing you revealed over a casual lunch. Even her friend Danielle didn't know the full story about her past. 'I wouldn't have done it if I'd realised.'

Talking about the kiss was somehow self-fulfilling, drawing her eyes to his lips unconsciously and reminding her of how they'd felt so warm and surprised against hers. Her mouth watered with the memory.

She forced her eyes upward only to collide with ones so intense and earnest they stole her breath.

'You remember it. I was beginning to wonder.'

'Of course I remember it. How many men in vehicle wrecks do you imagine I've kissed?'

'Not as many as me.'

'Wh—?'

'Mouth-to-mouth,' he said with a straight face,

but couldn't hold it. His smile undid all the tension of the past five minutes.

Her relief bubbled over. He was making this easier for her. How was it possible she was laughing again so soon after the awkwardness of just a moment ago?

Because this was Sam. 'That's it,' she said. 'That's what I was doing that night.'

He laughed. 'Yeah, let's go with that. Really good mouth-to-mouth.'

And just like that the awkwardness was back. At least for her. Sam didn't seem the slightest bit affected. His eyes strayed to the large parcel that contained the mirror, and he took shelter in a new subject. 'I just hope Mel likes it as much as you and I did,' he said.

Wow—how much had changed that talking about his wife was safer territory between them? 'She will. She'd have to be blind not to see how hard you've worked to get the perfect gift.' No man had ever made an effort to please her as Sam was making an effort to please his wife. 'She's very lucky.'

Her breath sucked in on a tiny gasp at her accidentally spoken words.

Sam lifted his eyes. 'Lucky?'

'That you're going to so much effort,' she stumbled. 'That you care enough to do…all of this…for her. You could have just gone with flowers.'

His lips twisted. 'She has no idea.'

'Then tell her,' Aimee said, locking her eyes

on his. 'Every woman deserves to know she's cherished.'

Sam frowned. 'I can't even *imagine* a conversation between us that would lead to that.'

Her eyebrows lifted. 'You don't talk?'

'Not like that.' He shook his head and his gaze flickered away. 'Not like this.'

Again her breath tightened. So it wasn't only she who found their time together easy and natural. 'That surprises me.'

His eyes lifted. 'Why?'

She shrugged. 'The Sam I met dangling off that highway…That's not a man I can imagine having difficulty communicating.'

'Mel's not really a talker.'

'Have you tried?'

His eyes shaded over. 'Repeatedly.'

She knew firsthand how frustrating it was to try and talk to someone who didn't reciprocate. Except in her case it had been more a case of Wayne not being a listener. He just hadn't stopped talking long enough for her to get a word in, and if she had, his reflex had been to disregard it.

Sam's gentle voice drew her eyes back to his. 'Has someone made you feel like that? Cherished?' The blue of his irises seemed to have grown richer.

Her mouth opened and then closed again without answer. That wasn't a question she could answer without embarrassing both of them.

Silent moments ticked by.

'Is our friendship one-way, Aimee?' he asked out of nowhere, shifting in his seat, not letting up with the eye-contact. Not angry, but rough enough that she winced—just slightly. 'You can ask me personal things but I can't ask you?'

'I...' That was actual hurt in his eyes. Or was she imagining it? Her pulse quickened. 'I've...I must have...'

He leaned forward. 'Everything I know about you I know from that one night on the mountain. Since then you haven't...invited personal conversation.'

Her heart beat in her throat. 'We just had one. About...' *The Kiss.*

'That wasn't personal. We were both involved. I'd like to know more about Aimee Leigh, about what makes her tick. You told those kids yesterday more about yourself in one hour than you've told me since we met.'

Old scars pinched tightly. In her household personal discussions had been discouraged lest they led to...you know...actual caring. She didn't *do* emotional risk. And opening up to this particular man would definitely be risky.

'Why?'

The question seemed to anger him. 'Because we're friends, Aimee. Or at least I think we are. I don't know.' He threw his hands into the air. 'Maybe we're not?'

Her chest tightened. *Friends.* 'We are. Of course we are.' *It's all we ever can be.*

'Then open up. Let me in.'

She matched the lift in his voice, though hers was tighter. 'I can't.'

He pressed his palms onto the table. 'Why not?'

'Because you're not mine to let in,' she half-shouted, her chest fixed with the pain of where they were about to go, of what she'd just admitted.

Neither of them moved.

For entire moments.

Even the birds around them held their breath. 'Opening up means something to me, Sam. I'm programmed to...' She shook her head. 'It means something.'

Her parents had cloistered her so tightly she didn't even know how to take a risk. How to dare to.

He leaned in. 'Aimee, I'm sorry. I'm not trying to be obtuse. I truly do not understand what you're saying.'

Her face pinched, and she recognised somewhere far away, deep inside, that this was not one of her finest moments. Her breath fluttered. 'I don't...open up...easily. But if I did it would be because we meant something to each other. And we don't have that kind of relationship.'

He squinted his confusion. 'You do mean something to me, Aimee.'

She groaned her frustration. 'I'm not talking about friendship, Sam.' Lord, could he not hear her?

He shook his head, as though it might rattle all

the pieces together into an understandable shape. 'Are you saying that you only open up with some-one if you're in a relationship?'

She just stared at him.

'What? So I'm either in or I'm out?' he grated. 'There's nothing in between?'

'You're not someone I could let in just a little bit, Sam.' *Please understand what I'm saying. Please.*

He blinked at her. 'I don't want to be out.'

So innocent in its utterance, so painful in its intent. 'But you *can't* be in.'

And finally it dawned in his eyes. What she was trying so hard not to say. He sat back and took a deep, slow breath. 'This is about Melissa.'

She flung her hands in the air. 'Of course it is.'

'You're keeping a distance because of her?'

'I'm keeping the distance you should be keep-ing, Sam.'

That hit him hard. The colour fled from his face. But he didn't make excuses. He didn't defend himself. And his next words surprised her. 'What have they done to you?'

Two seconds ago he had been under exami-nation. Now he was turning the spotlight on her again. 'Who?'

'Your family. The men in your past. They've made you this all-or-nothing woman. A person who can't even have friendships without rules. Is that truly the world you come from?'

'They've done nothing.' Though that wasn't strictly true. Wayne had run off most of her male friends and dressed it up as his great devotion and focus on just being with her. And her father had been the same with her mother up until the day Lisbet Leigh threw his belongings out in the street. Both of those men and the lessons they'd taught her had had an impact on her. 'I still have values, Sam. They haven't changed just because I've struck out on my own.' If anything they'd crystallised.

'You pursued this friendship, Aimee.'

She sighed, because it was true. She had opened the door for all of this that day at the awards ceremony. It had seemed so doable at the time.

'But you're saying it can only be one-way?' he went on. 'Or superficial?'

God, how could such an intelligent man be so blind? Damn him for making her explain. 'You have a *wife,* Sam.'

He threw his palms up again. 'I'm not suggesting anything illicit, Aimee. There are degrees. Friends have a different level of intimacy. A different role.'

Aimee surged to her feet and slapped her fists on the table, leaning across it. 'Not for me. If I let you in then you will be *in.* Do you understand me? Is that a complication you want?'

Sam stared at the dignity and passion in her eyes. He almost chased the conversation to its natural conclusion, followed the white rabbit deep down into the hole, because for one blazing second—*yes*—he did want that complication.

Very much. But Aimee was right: getting closer to her emotionally wasn't going to do either of them any favours. He should be admiring the strength of her character, or cursing the lack of his own, but all he could think about was that this amazing human being was apparently off-limits to him.

And, God help him, he wanted to be *in*.

'So that's how this has to be? A careful distance between us?' he said.

'Don't you think that's wise?' Aimee slumped back onto her side of the bench and into the shaft of dappled light streaming down through the tangle of flowers overhead. It made her mop of blonde hair shimmer like a halo, like some angelic being. But all that did was make him feel more like playing the devil.

'No. Not if it means I can't get to know you.' She flinched, and he regretted causing it, but Aimee was fast becoming one of the important people in his life and her opting out was not on the cards. 'I like you, Aimee. I like how you think so differently to me in many ways but on the essential things we're in tune. I don't like being told that I can't be friends with you just because of Melissa.'

But he didn't like that he'd referred to the woman he'd married as 'just', either. And he *really* didn't like the resentment that had started oozing through the moment Melissa had become an obstacle between him and getting to know Aimee better. He frowned internally. He'd been working so hard on managing that ugly, unreasonable side of himself, but apparently it was alive and well.

Aimee lifted one prosaic brow and the corners of her mouth tightened. 'It's not actually your call, Sam, whether I'm friends with you or not, or what kind of a friend I am. If that's what you're expecting, then…'

She leaned down for her own shopping bags and her reach had a tremor in it. *Ugh, idiot!* She was breaking away from under the controlling thumb of her family and here he was going all caveman on her. He rushed in to undo his damage.

'I respect you, Aimee.' That stilled her fingers just as they started to pull on the handles of her bags. 'And that goes for whatever decision you choose to make about this. About us.'

She straightened up and brought her green eyes back to his, and he hated the caution he saw there. Partly because he'd caused it, and partly because he knew she was never going to tell him who'd put it there in the first place. One of a thousand things he'd never get to know about Aimee Leigh if she got her way.

He folded his arms in front of him on the table and leaned towards her. 'Keeping our friendship shallow feels like a crime against nature. But I'm not about to force the issue. I know you well enough to know that you'll walk if I do. Like it or not, you're a part of my life now, Aimee, so I don't want you to do that.' He wasn't about to look too closely at why. Not today at least. He smiled and hoped it seemed genuine. 'So, even though I don't agree with you, I'll take whatever you'll give me.'

Her eyes darkened and dropped briefly, but when they rose they were flat. 'I like and respect you, too, Sam. But you have a wife. She's where your emotional investment should be.'

She was right. Of course she was. And Lord knew if ever a marriage needed emotional investment it was his and Mel's.

But he still hated it.

He shook off the growling doubts in his stomach, stood when he should have been reassuring her, and waved a hand towards the bright fabric sticking out of his bag. 'Come on. How long has it been since you flew a kite?'

Kites were superficial. Harmless and pretty. She couldn't be suspicious of a bit of recreational fun, right?

But her eyes could.

'I've never flown one. I think my mother was afraid of friction burns on my hands.'

A long-dormant part of him deep inside roused, lifted its slumberous head. Aimee had been so protected from life…The things she must not know… The things that he could teach her…

If she was his to teach.

But all he said was, 'Come on. Time to add a new life-skill to your repertoire.'

Sam's heart was simultaneously warmed and saddened by the enjoyment Aimee got from her lesson. His urge to protect her clashed headlong with his anger at the selfishness of her parents—raising her in an over-cautious bubble and robbing her of simple childhood joys.

Like flying a kite.

She set off again, in a long-limbed gallop across the open parkland, with the fuchsia fabric eel trailing behind her, lifting higher, flirting with the current. This time it caught and held, and she jogged to a halt and looked back at him across the foreshore, with triumph in her whole body as it climbed.

'It's up!' she cried in astonishment, bouncing on the spot, returning her eyes to the feminine kite wavering and folding in the air high above her.

'She's like an alien,' Sam muttered as he jogged across to her, his own yellow and black kite in his hands. A big-brained alien who existed on learning new things.

'If she starts to drop,' he called out, 'pull on the line. If she veers left, you pull right...'

In under a minute Sam was by her side, staring up into the electric blue above the park, his hawk kite dominating the sky, expertly keeping his strings from tangling in Aimee's.

'You're good!' She laughed as her eel tumbled momentarily.

Sam reached one hand over on top of hers and showed her how to moderate its altitude. Her hands were warm and soft and fitted perfectly in his. He had to force himself to let go. 'I flew kites as a kid. It's like riding a bike. You never really forget.'

'I never learned that, either.' She squealed as the eel cut to the left sharply, but she'd already started correcting it.

'You have good instincts.' He smiled.

'I'm not exactly tearing up the sky.' She laughed. 'I'm too scared to move out of my safe little orbit.'

'You just need the right motivation. Watch out.' A flick of his wrist turned the sharp-winged hawk back towards the eel and he cut it back and forth on her tail like a predator toying with its prey. Its two long ribbons streamed like twin vapour-trails behind.

'Quit it!' Aimee grumbled, laughing.

'Make me.'

She kicked into top gear then, weaving her kite ahead of his, trying to anticipate whatever stunt he'd pull next, her frown pronounced as she concentrated on besting him. She wasn't bad, but half an hour's experience was never going to beat a lifetime love of the skies, and he had plenty of easy time to glance back at what the eel's pilot was doing.

A light sheen of sweat glistened on Aimee's golden forehead and determination blazed in her heaven-lifted gaze. His eyes dropped to her full mouth. Lingered.

'Does biting your lip help?' he teased.

The guilty lip sprang free and she smiled,

broad and brilliant, but didn't take her eyes off
his hawk. 'Yes. It improves my aerodynamics.'

Immediately his mind was filled with thoughts
and images that she'd have been horrified to
know he harboured. He shook them loose and
disguised them with a laugh. 'Interesting tech-
nique.'

Above, Sam wound his hawk in tight circles
around the eel, trapping it in the spiral of the
twin-tails, but she broke free and let herself soar
high above him, before circling back around and
down to meet him from the side. He dodged away
and twisted back, to race the eel through the sky.

The two of them moved in parallel, tightly
synchronised, and Sam's glance ping-ponged
down to see what Aimee's hands were going
to do next before shooting back up to watch his
hawk respond.

Where she ducked, he dived. When she turned
he was right there with her, mirroring her every
move.

Her radiant gaze grew large as the beauty and
sensuality of the airshow overtook her. Her lips
fell open and she sighed. He felt it in his gut more
than heard it. Sam took his chance, tightening his
strings and bringing the headstrong hawk back
under tight control, curling close around the eel
but never quite tangling with it. The two kites
danced in dreamy synchronicity across the blue
canvas sky.

Wild, open, limitless. A place where anything,
any future, was possible. His breath grew short.

For one brief moment he raced the hawk ahead of her, hovered in space as her eel caught up, and then twisted in freefall to touch it in a slow-motion aerial kiss before falling away in a showy controlled dive.

Beside him, Aimee gasped.

He steered the hawk back into an ascent and his focus flicked to her, met her gaze head-on. Wide-eyed. Flushed.

Utterly dismayed.

He fumbled his climb, and the strings were yanked meanly from Aimee's hands as the two kites tangled, tipped, and plummeted in a twisted mess to the hard ground in the distance, their sensual skirmish terminally interrupted.

I'll take whatever you'll give me.

That was what he'd said back at the little cafeteria, and he'd meant it to be kind. Some sort of compromise between what he wanted—to really get to know her—and what she needed—to keep a safe emotional gulf between them. But all it did was hurt and mirror her own *patheticism* back to her. Not even a real word—but it summed her situation up perfectly so she was going with it. She was taking whatever *he* would give *her*.

How had she found herself in this situation—again? She marched resolutely back towards the car, her chest balled tight around her anger and pain.

Anger at herself.

Pain because he'd never be able to touch her for real.

What was she prepared to give him? *Everything.* But she wanted everything in return. Not a friend. Not a shopping buddy. She wanted someone she could curl up with at night, see the wonders of the world with, and whose brain she could mine for useless information. She wanted someone to admire and appreciate and get jealous over. She wanted someone to wander the markets with or sail a boat or fly a kite. Or cheer for at an awards ceremony. All perfectly legitimately.

She wanted someone like Sam. She *deserved* someone like Sam. And it was a bit of a first in her life to be thinking that way. But all those things were way, way more than he was free to give.

And so Sam playing kissing-kites had done nothing but mess with her head and cut her deep down inside where she never let anyone go.

'Aimee… Stop.'

'Someone will steal your kites,' she threw back over her stiff shoulder, picking up pace as the park got smaller behind them.

'They'll have to untangle them first.'

Her smile stretched her skin tight. Even his sharp wit got up her nose. Why couldn't he be an egotist? Or as thick as two planks? Was he not even the slightest bit muddled by what had just happened back in the skies? By that little aerial seduction?

Did he not even have the decency to be vaguely rattled?

'Aimee. Please.'

Her feet slowed. Shuffled. Stopped. But she didn't turn around. Either he'd see how mad she was or he'd see the confusion in her eyes, and she didn't want either. She clenched her fists. 'I've got somewhere to be, Sam. I'm not at your disposal all day.'

'You're angry with me.'

Her eyes drifted shut and she turned slowly, marshalling her expression. 'I'm not angry with you. I'm just angry at...' *The universe. The timing.* '...this whole situation.'

'It was nothing. It wasn't supposed to be anything.'

That meant he knew it was something. Her mouth dried up.

He lifted his hands either side of him. 'I just wanted you to have the chance to fly a kite.'

'Why?'

'Because you never have. That seems wrong.'

'Why is it your job to fix the ills of my past?'

He frowned. 'Because...' But his words evaporated and his shoulders sagged. 'I don't know, Aimee. I just wanted to see your face the first time you got the kite up. I wanted to give you that.'

She stared at him. It was a nice thing to do, and it *was* just kites. But then it wasn't. 'So what was with the kite foreplay?'

It was a risk. She watched his face closely for

signs of total bemusement, for a hint that this was all in her head and totally one-sided and she'd just made a complete fool of herself. Or for the defensiveness of a man caught out.

She got neither.

'I don't know,' he murmured, frowning and stepping closer. 'It just happened. And it was kind of…' She tipped her head as he grasped for the right words. 'Beautiful. Organic. It didn't feel wrong.'

It *had* been beautiful and it had started so naturally, but it was wrong. It had felt too good so it had to be wrong. She shoved her hands deep into the pockets of her sweatshirt and took a deep, slow breath. 'This is how we're always going to go, Sam. Even something ordinary like flying a kite becomes—' *loaded* '—unordinary.'

He ruffled long fingers through his hair and stared at her. 'So maybe that's just us? Why don't we just…allow for it?'

Allow for it? 'How?'

He stopped in front of her, looking down with deep, calm eyes. 'It is what it is, Aimee. Neither one of us is going to act on it, so do we really need to stress about it? We could just accept that there's an…attraction…between us, and then just move past it.'

Her lips twisted along with the torsion in her gut. 'You make it sound so simple.'

'I'm sure we're not the first two people who have accidental chemistry.'

Except it wasn't just chemistry for her. Her

mind was involved. Her heart. And that made it very complicated.

'What just happened with the kites…' he started. 'I feel comfortable around you, Aimee. Relaxed. It just happened. I'll be on my guard from now on so that it doesn't happen again.'

Her chest hurt. 'What kind of friendship is that going to make? If we're both constantly guarding our words and actions?' *Our hearts.*

His broad shoulders lifted and fell, but she couldn't tell if it was a shrug or a sigh. 'Our kind.'

Sam's defeat was contagious. Her eyes dropped to the ground.

'Come on. We have an hour before we're due back. Let's go rescue the kites and then go back to the café for that interview.'

The interview. Did either of them believe that excuse any more? But the pages of her book were already established neutral territory between them, so it was good to have it to retreat to.

Just accept the attraction…

Aimee shook her head. He was so easy to believe. He was so certain that this was a good idea. Sam had no doubt that he could put aside whatever this was simmering away between them, and maybe he could.

But could she?

CHAPTER TEN

AIMEE re-read the opening to the oral history spread out on the hotel table before her and stared at the words as though they were prophecy.

She'd first met Coraline McMahon as an elderly woman from the suburbs of Melbourne, but the Cora she was meeting now was fifteen, beautiful, running barefoot and wild in her home on the Isle of Man. Cora had set her cap at tearaway Danny McMahon from a very early age—a young man idolised by the boys, dreamed of by the girls, and *tsked* about by their parents alike, which had only made him all the more desirable. Dark and bold and charismatic. She'd fallen hard and irrevocably for Danny, but he'd left her behind when he'd enlisted in the Second World War.

Broken-hearted. Fifteen.

Pregnant.

Within weeks a shamed Cora had been married off to Danny's younger brother Charley: the responsible one, the tolerant one, the one willing to raise his brother's child to avoid a family scandal. They'd had a sound sort of marriage, living in the McMahon household while the war raged on, until the day Danny got a foot blown off and limped home to a hero's welcome.

'Ugh.' Aimee dropped the sheets of her transcribed story onto the tabletop and slid down further on her chair to study the ceiling.

Every day.

Every day Cora had struggled with wanting a man she couldn't have. Living under the same roof. Watching him making a slow life for himself. It had broken Charley's heart, watching her try to hide it. She'd never so much as touched Danny again, but breathing the same air as him had tarnished her soul and her husband's—even after he'd packed them all up and shipped them to Australia to escape his older brother's influence.

Aimee's subconscious shrieked at her to pay attention. To what, though? What was the right message to take from Cora's cautionary tale?

Was it counsel against the pain of spending time with someone she wanted but could never have? Or a reminder of how damaging it could be to any future relationship she might form? Or was it a living warning about not seizing the moment, of settling for someone less than you wanted? Cora had lived seventy years with second-best, faithful, loyal, accepting Charley McMahon. Yet he'd married her because she was pregnant with his brother's child. Pressured by his parents. And he'd lived his life knowing her heart truly belonged to his brother.

No matter the great affection that had eventually grown between them, each of them lived had long lives knowing that neither was the other's first choice.

That was just…awful.

And yet their story was going in her book. Coraline McMahon had willingly given her life to the brother she didn't love. She'd done the right thing by her family, her son, on her own merit. She hadn't been swayed by the fact that it was the wrong thing for her. Outwardly it smacked of passivity, but there was great strength in the way she'd taken her unplanned future by the scruff and fashioned a reasonable life for herself, and that made her story perfect for *Navigators.*

She'd owned her choices and she lived with the consequences. For ever.

But…oh…how it had hurt her.

Aimee remembered the cloudy agony in Cora's eyes as she'd relived the day they'd trundled away from the McMahon home with their meagre belongings stacked around them. Told her about the momentary eye-contact she'd shared with a broken and war-shocked Danny, standing respectfully to the rear of the group farewelling his brother's family.

Bare seconds locked together. Her first and only glimpse of the saturated sorrow in his eyes. Realising he'd loved her after all.

How had she managed, never seeing him again, never speaking to him…? Aimee studied the yellowed photograph of Cora and her son aboard the ship they'd boarded for Australia. Seeing Danny every single day in the dark eyes of their son?

Was that a comfort or a kind of torture?

She squared up the bundled pages that captured Cora's story and refastened the elastic band around them tight, sealing in all the heartbreak. The cover title was the widow's final words to her on the last day of their interviews: *This Too Shall Pass*.

Except Aimee felt certain it had never passed for Coraline McMahon. She was strong and honourable, and hadn't been afraid to reinvent herself for her son's sake, but she'd carry the secret pain of Danny's loss to her grave.

Aimee slid the documents back into their file and swallowed back tears. Would she have the same strength of character? Endurance? Would she grow to accept Sam's unavailability or, like Cora, would her heart form a callus around the wound so that she could survive?

'Phone, Aimee…'

She jumped at Sam's voice, so close behind her, and reached for her mobile as the special ring-tone he'd recorded on her phone the day before repeated itself.

'Phone, Aimee…'

But just as she went to accept his call she paused, glanced at Cora's notes, and then at the hotel wall between their suites. She tuned in to the heart that hammered in Pavlovian response just to the sound of Sam's voice. The cell-deep anticipation that excited her blood.

'Phone, Aimee…'

And she let it go to voicemail.

She opened the door, expecting hotel staff to collect her bags, and found Sam there, instead, a deep scowl marring his handsome face and fire sparking in his eyes. Her stomach clenched.

'Why are you leaving?' he said.

Because it's not healthy for me to be around you, like this. Because I need to remove myself from the temptation of touching you.

'You don't need me for this afternoon's meetings so I might as well fly out today.' *Without you.*

'But what difference does one more night make?'

Her whole body stiffened up. That was not an easy question to answer. If he knew what she'd be wanting to do right through that night… What she'd wanted to do that first night, with a head full of images of him in his towel… Or last night, fuelled by sensual dream images of his strong, lithe fabric hawk kite twisting around her… How long she'd lain awake taking herself through the mental pros and cons of rolling out of bed and tiptoeing next door… How hard it had been to finally settle on not doing it…

Her arms crept around her front. 'None, to you. But I'd like to get home now that I'm not needed. I've done my part for your department.'

It was more defensive than she'd meant it, but that couldn't be helped. Being strong had to start somewhere.

He frowned. 'You have. You've been amazing. I just…'

'What, Sam?'

'Are you leaving because of yesterday? Because of what I said on your recorder?'

There was nothing too controversial about what they'd recorded at the café. But 'yesterday' could only mean the kites. She tossed her hair back. 'I'm leaving because I'm done.' *Totally.* 'And because staying has absolutely no purpose.'

His eyes smouldered the way they had at the end of their kite-flying. He was busting to say more, but even he had to see the sense in not hurting each other any further.

Aimee's skin stretched to snapping point as they stood there, silently.

'So…good luck this afternoon.' She stood back to close her door.

'I'll call you. When I get back to Hobart.'

Her heart squeezed. 'Why?'

His scowl bisected his handsome face. 'Your book. Don't we need to finish the interview?'

The book. The last remaining thread between them. A totally fake thread.

She pressed her fingernails into her palms. 'I think I got everything I needed yesterday.'

'I'll call you. To be sure.'

She'd seen him angry, amused, confused, delighted. But she'd never seen Sam so…adrift.

Cutting him completely free just wasn't something she could do at this very second. She needed more strength for that.

She sighed. 'Okay.'

No one said she had to answer his call.

The banks of the Derwent were busy as always—even for a week day. Small watercraft under billowing sails glided along its gleaming surface, and presumptuous ducks busied themselves nearby, waiting for any scraps that might tumble from Aimee's lunch. Parallel pairs of prams pushed by athletic mums dominated the shared pathway and cyclists had to rumble onto the grass to go around them.

Aimee sat on her comfortable bench, tucked back into a recess in the thick foliage edging the pathway, munching absently on her chicken sandwich, her eyes very much lost amongst the boats out on the channel. Glorious golden rays of sun sprinkled down, warming all they touched.

Was there anything more restorative? A productive morning in Hobart's research library, a simple lunch by the Derwent and a silent mind. A rare treat after the emotion of the past few days.

Aimee sighed and sipped her apple juice.

A clutch of power-walking nannas passed her, chatting across each other like the ducks grumbling around her feet, and she followed them with her eyes as she ate. She missed Danielle. Not that they'd ever been power-walking-type friends, but she missed having someone to chat to, to share work with, since her friend had gone on a month's leave back to New Zealand.

Maybe that was what she needed? Some more friends. Broader horizons. New people. Non-Sam people.

As if just thinking his name had made him manifest, the gaggle of fast-moving nannas split like a cell, dividing around two people strolling towards her secluded corner of riverbank in the distance, then reformed behind them.

Her tasty chicken turned to ash in her mouth.

Sam.

With his wife.

They stopped in the distance and watched the boats go by, the downward tilt of Sam's head indicating he was listening intently. Eager to see her after his three days away.

Aimee's body reacted as immediately and inappropriately as it always did to the sight of Sam: tightening, anticipating. Going all gooey. But for the first time it wasn't him that dominated her focus.

Melissa was as small and slim as she remembered from the confused chaos of the A10. But she was better lit in the golden noon light than she had been in the dimness of early morning on the mountain, and infinitely better dressed in businesswear rather than the running pants and sweater she'd had on that cold morning. Dark hair tumbled around her shoulders and seemed to blaze red in the sunlight.

She was…radiant.

Aimee's heart pattered harder, and she dropped her eyes rather than be caught staring. Not that Melissa would have a clue who she was. But Sam would, if he turned around and saw her. Her mouth dried.

She hadn't expected Melissa to be so lovely. She'd built an image of a fusty scientist gadding around in a lab coat stained by God knew what in a poor attempt to diminish her. What kind of cosmic injustice was this, that she should get Sam's heart *and* be beautiful, too?

But of course he would pick someone beautiful. Ethereal.

She risked a glance up again. Sam's back was still to her. But she recognised that posture, the slope of his shoulders.

They stood barely separated, barely touching, and watched the boats. Then Melissa turned and peered up at her husband with such unmasked adoration it stole Aimee's breath. Even from a distance she knew that this was not the face of a woman who was unhappy in her marriage. And right then another convenient myth crumbled. She'd built an image of two mutually unhappy people trying to make a doomed marriage work. It had suited her to think that Sam's dissatisfaction wasn't one-sided.

Because that made him a better man.

As she watched he lifted a hand to stroke an errant lock of hair from Melissa's face, but Aimee was too far away to see the details of her expression. Did his wife's eyes drift shut in bliss at that tiny contact? Did her lips fall open on a tiny breath the way hers would have? Certainly her body seemed to sway towards his. Would Sam have *that* smile on his face—the gentle half-twist that matched the warm glow in his gaze? Would he still be smiling as he leaned in to kiss her?

Melissa stretched up onto her toes and Aimee dropped her head, forcing her voyeuristic gaze to the pathway, her stomach churning, her lips tight, her heart screaming.

Damn him.

And damn herself.

She'd fooled herself into believing—stupidly—that they were staying together out of some kind of obligation, that they were physically together but emotionally apart. Where was the obligation in Melissa's devoted gaze just then? Where was the emotional separation in the way Sam gently brushed her cheek with his knuckle? Even faking it wouldn't be that convincing.

She forced her rampant heart back into some kind of regular metre, her breathing easing. But her chest was still tight.

It was not fake. There was love there. Lots and lots of it.

Did it make her a bad person that she really couldn't find it in herself to be happy for Sam? She wanted that love for herself.

When she dared to glance up they were gone, back the way they'd come.

She sagged back into her bench, spared the hideousness of having them bump into her, fresh out of that touchy-feely display. She wasn't sure she could look Sam in the eye and not cry.

She wasn't sure she could look Melissa in the eye at all.

Thinking of her as 'the wife', or imagining her in shabby jogging pants with a severe ponytail, or in that stained lab coat, or as a faceless, nameless person, had all been futile attempts to depersonalise the woman behind the wedding ring. To somehow make it okay that she was coveting someone else's husband.

She didn't need a commandment to tell her it was wrong. She knew it was wrong. For so many reasons.

But try telling her straining pulse that.

She tossed what was left of her sandwich down to the ducks and ignored the fat little birds that raced in to demolish it, staring off in the direction Sam and Melissa had gone.

Delusion, thy name is Aimee.

Somewhere deep down she'd seriously convinced herself that Sam was miserable, holding onto his marriage out of some misguided honour. Because that had made her feel less *dis*honourable about the feelings for him that she was harbouring.

But he was doing just fine in the job of getting past whatever speed bump his marriage had hit, judging by what she'd just seen. If he'd rushed back from Melbourne to stroll the riverbank with his wife on a work day then they weren't exactly at loggerheads.

Which meant Aimee was distracting Sam from a perfectly *healthy* relationship—not a fatally flawed one.

And she knew exactly what else that meant.

Bundling up her rubbish and her empty juice container, and tucking her research under her arm, she hurried down the cycle path in the opposite direction from Melissa and Sam.

There were some fates you just didn't tempt.

CHAPTER ELEVEN

'WHAT do you mean, we're done?'

Aimee stared at him, wringing her fingers under the café table. 'I've got what I need for the book.'

Sam's beautiful face folded. 'So that's it?'

She took a careful breath. 'Your history is nearly complete. Today should be our last interview. It's a good time to wind things up.'

'Including our friendship?'

Yes. 'No. We'll still see each other.' She frowned at the lie. 'From time to time.'

His lips thinned. 'Christmas and birthdays?'

She reinforced her back against the hurt in his eyes. 'Sam…'

'Aimee, we already had this conversation.'

Every part of her wanted to cave, but she forced a resolute expression to her face.

He frowned. 'I thought your book was…'

Just an excuse?

It had been since the beginning, if she was honest with herself.

But he changed tack. 'I thought our friendship was about more than just your book.'

God, why was it so hard to keep things professional when he was sitting there looking so wounded. She forced herself to remember the blazing adoration in Melissa's upturned face. 'Sure it is.'

'Why don't I believe you?'

She took a breath, as though it would help her lie better. 'Our friendship was forged under extraordinary circumstances. Maybe it wasn't meant to outlive that night on the A10.'

'You can't seriously believe that?'

She met his accusation with blank eyes. Not defending or reacting. 'You said you respected me.'

Three little lines appeared at the bridge of his nose. He looked as if he wanted to disagree. But he didn't. How could he, in good faith? 'I do. Of course I do.'

'Then respect my decision. I think we're done...' She squeezed her fists. 'On all fronts.'

He leaned in closer. 'Aimee, why?'

But just then a shadow loomed over their table. They both looked up into a startlingly familiar face. Sam leaped to his feet, his expression annoyed and grateful at the same time. Maybe he needed a moment to regroup. She'd really thrown him, if the paleness of his face was any indication.

'Aimee, this is my big brother Anthony. Tony, this is Aimee Leigh.'

Aimee smiled past her surprise, slid her hand into Anthony's, and lifted her eyes to his. So this was Sam's infamous big brother. He was very definitely family.

'Your expression tells me I wasn't expected,' he said to her, and glared at Sam.

Sam shrugged it off, turned to Aimee. 'I figured it could be useful getting a family member's perspective on me. For your oral history.'

Oh, the timing. She'd just told him the history was finished. But Anthony didn't deserve to get dragged into their sorry mess. *The sins of the brother...*

'Ah...very useful,' she agreed. And she wasn't entirely lying. He'd be a good buffer between them today, the first time they'd been alone since she flew back to Hobart. Flew away from her out-of-control feelings for Sam. She'd said yes to coffee today with the intention of saying goodbye in person. Respectfully.

She hadn't expected the sledgehammer between the ribs on seeing him again, nor his obvious hurt at her farewell. A mountain of sadness sagged through her. 'I'm sorry you've been roped in, though, Tony.'

Those broad shoulders shrugged. 'Not a problem. I was visiting Sammy anyway. Might as well eat and talk.'

'You're staring, Aimee,' Sam murmured.

Heat chased up her neck as they stood to cross to a larger booth. She wished she could extricate herself right now and flee. 'I'm sorry. I'm just… You two are similar, but I'm just trying to pinpoint why.' There was a lot about them that wasn't alike—their eye colour, their individual features—yet the overall picture… 'It's very interesting.'

He and Tony slid into the booth in much the same way, and then addressed the waitress with the same tone, the same courteous head-tilt. They even laughed the same.

'Amoeba interesting,' Sam clarified for his brother. 'Aimee's a student of human nature.'

Tony stretched along the booth, one muscled arm lying across its back, and smiled at her across the table. 'Stare away. I have no problem being scrutinised by a beautiful woman.'

Awkwardness rushed in to displace the burbling curiosity. Her mouth fell shut. Tony's self-confidence should have been appealing—it clearly was to the waitress, who appeared with their coffees, got hers mixed up with Sam's in a daze, and then stood hovering for unnecessarily long—but Aimee couldn't rustle up more than a professional curiosity in the man sitting across from her.

Unlike the man at her side. Even without looking at him Aimee could feel Sam's presence. The way he studied them both. His badly disguised interest.

That made her frown.

She reached across and automatically swapped the short black in front of her for the decaf latte the waitress had mistakenly put down in front of Sam. He tossed her a sugar lump, then waited until she had stirred her coffee before using the same spoon to dissolve his one lump in the small, steaming cup of dark, fragrant goodness.

Tony's eyes followed every action.

In that moment everything got incredibly *real*. Having Sam's closest friend and brother here with them was only a half-step from having Melissa sitting here, watching. Drawing conclusions.

Judging.

She wanted to cry out that this was a goodbye meeting.

Both of them had been living in their personal little Sam/Aimee bubble—to the exclusion of anyone else—anyone to reflect back to them what they were doing. How they must appear.

It was a blissfully protected way to run a relationship.

She stiffened and faltered and pressed her hands down beneath the table. Not a relationship. *A friendship.* Not even that…

'So, Aimee…' Tony said, then paused to take a sip of his long macchiato. 'Sammy tells me he rescued you off a mountain a while back?'

She looked sideways at Sam who glared at his brother. For some reason that shocked her—that he would have mentioned her at all, let alone the details of her rescue. For so long those hours had been a private thing between the two of them. A special thing. Maybe it was better that it wasn't private any more. Maybe Tony was doing her a favour with his sharp eyes and interest.

She dragged her eyes back to him. 'Yes. A lucky day for me.'

In more ways than one.

'Don't get me wrong,' Tony said, striving for normalcy and doing his best to ignore his still glaring brother. 'It wasn't like he was gossiping. Sam has always…decompressed…with me after particularly nasty jobs. It helps him deal with it all.'

That drew her eyes back to Sam's. 'I was *particularly nasty*?' she asked, lost in his blue depths. For some reason the fact that he'd needed to talk to his brother about her touched her way deep down inside.

He met her intensity and as always her insides squirmed. 'Your situation was. You were easy.'

'In the nicest possible way,' Tony cut in, glaring at his brother's rudeness. Though a hint of speculation strained his voice.

That got Aimee's attention. Sam was a married man, and she was sitting here making cow eyes at him. In front of his brother. She forced her focus back onto Tony with a forced laugh. 'Thank you. You must be the chivalrous one of the family.'

That earned a smile from both brothers—though Sam's was still tight—and the awkward moment lurched past.

They chatted for a bit longer, until Aimee bent to rustle her mini-recorder from her handbag to start the interview she imagined Tony expected.

As she straightened she caught the tail-end of a meaningful look between the brothers. Sam didn't look all that happy.

'I've just...' He fumbled in his pocket for his phone, avoiding her eyes. 'Phone call. Won't be long.'

And without so much as a smile of apology he slid out of the booth and headed for the door.

Well, that had been slick. *Not.* And entirely unconvincing, judging by the confused frown on Aimee's face—and the amused smirk on his brother's—as he'd bolted out of there.

Sam threw a right into the service alley next to the restaurant and rested his back against the wall, pocketing his phone. He'd only thought this plan up late Sunday night, when he'd discovered Tony would be in town this week. Bad timing, given his trip with Aimee, but then again Melbourne had given him a few days to think about it—to change his mind three times and then change it back again.

But he wasn't used to this sort of thing—opportunism, artifice—that was why his exit from the café had been extra lame.

Maybe that was why the whole thing with Melissa was doing his head in, too. He just wasn't cut out for all this...subterfuge.

Ten days ago, wanting Aimee to meet his brother had been just an excuse to see her again. The whole book thing. He'd thought the cover was pretty brilliant. But midway through the Melbourne trip—right after the kite incident—he'd come up with a whole new reason for the visit.

Tony was his favourite brother—no matter the difficulties they'd had between them in the past or the occasional awkwardness of the present—and he wouldn't trust Aimee with anyone else. Not because his brother wouldn't make a move on her, but because when he did—and he absolutely would—Sam trusted she'd be in safe hands. Tony had made some bad choices as a younger man, but he was rock solid now. The sort of man you'd trust your daughter with. Or your best friend.

Or someone else.

His brother was smart. He'd know the book excuse was fabricated. He believed that he was simply being set up. He had no clue that he'd originally been an accomplice to Sam's attempts to see Aimee. But then he and his brother had always had the same taste in women.

They'd be good for each other. Tony was overdue for his own happy ending. He'd tried and failed with several women in the past decade, never quite finding the right one. Eventually he'd just given up. Aimee had *right one* written all over her in bright, talented letters.

Maybe right enough to sway his brother from his lonely path.

She was crying out for someone good in her life. Someone who'd treasure her but not smother

her. Support her. And love her the way she wanted to be loved.

Deserved to be.

Thrusting Aimee at Tony had churned his stomach, but it was kind of like controlling a climbing fall. You knew it was going to hurt, but if you did it the right way then you minimised the injury when you hit bottom. He had nothing to offer Aimee himself, but this way she'd remain in his life—albeit in the periphery.

Given what it seemed she'd come here today to say, it wasn't a moment too soon.

A deep sigh racked his tight body.

So why did it feel so wrong when his head knew it was a good plan? Why had he had to force himself from that booth to leave her alone with the man he trusted above all others? It was just an introduction, just a chance for them to talk, to find a connection with each other. For two outstanding people to meet. Tony would do the rest.

Yet his brain was the only part of his body not screaming at him to go back in, to undo what he'd just done. To grab Aimee's hand and haul her out of the booth, out of the restaurant, and get her the hell out of Tony's orbit. And maybe not stop hauling her until they found themselves a remote, lawless mountain somewhere. Far from Hobart. Far from his wedding vows. Far from his family. Far from society's expectations.

Far from the total mess he'd made of his life.

Where they could just...*be*. Together.

He fished his wedding band out from under his T-shirt and stared at it. *Yeah, and if the moon was a balloon...*

He pressed his lips together and glanced at his watch. Ten minutes was enough. If Tony hadn't caught her attention in that time then he was off his game and didn't deserve the chance.

He pushed away from the wall.

There was something so staged, so *un-Sam* about the way he'd just sprinted out of the restaurant. He was never awkward. Only ever infuriatingly collected.

Aimee turned her attention back to Tony and ran headlong into his best *How're you doin'?* smile.

A hard twist bit low in her gut deep inside, and her mortified eyes drifted shut.

This was a set-up.

The bite turned into a rancid ache and spread around to her lower back.

Sam was setting her up with his brother. *Sam.* The man she had such complex feelings for. This was his answer to the rogue attraction between them—throw another obstacle into the mix. She smiled tightly, and scrabbled around for something harmless to say, but inside her mind screamed.

Genius! If his wife wasn't enough to head off her feelings, what on earth made him think his brother would be? No matter how handsome.

Or was he stacking the deck on his side?

She slid the digital recorder into the centre of the table—firmly. The interview was pathetically paper-thin as excuses went, but she was going to cling to it to the end. It had served her so well until now. Tony might be here for a set-up, but she absolutely did not have to play.

'So... You grew up in a big family with Sam,' she started. 'What was that like?'

'Subtlety has never been his strong suit,' he said, leaning forward.

A cryptic kind of answer to her question, but Aimee didn't let that put her off. 'It's hard for me to imagine, coming from a one-child family.'

'He means well, Aimee.'

She frowned. Were they having the same conversation? 'Was he competitive as a child?'

'I'm no more interested in a hook-up than you are. No offence.'

That got her attention. She abandoned her pretence and braved Tony's direct gaze. 'Then why are you here?'

'Honestly? I was curious.'

'About what?'

'About this random woman that keeps popping up in his conversations. About why he'd try and set me up with one of his friends after all this time. About what made you so special.'

Her heart thumped. 'And now?'

His brown eyes darkened and he leaned forward even further. 'Now I'm even more curious. The two of you made coffee like an old married couple just then. Perfectly choreographed.'

She laughed and tried to make it light. 'We've shared a lot of coffees.'

'Obviously.'

The speculation in his eyes bothered her. And the judgement. She pressed her lips together. 'But that's all we've shared, if that's what you're getting at.' If you didn't count an ill-considered kiss and some sky-high kite action.

'I'm not getting at anything. I'm just trying to understand.'

The intense scrutiny burned. 'Would he try to set me up with you if there was something going on?'

Tony's face twisted. 'That's absolutely what he would do. He's Sam.'

The man had a point. 'Maybe he just thinks we'd…get along.'

'I guarantee you we would.' Speculation glittered in his eyes. 'But I don't think that's why he did it.'

The strangest tug-of-war—between liking Tony and disliking him—nagged at her. It made her already tight body ratchet up a notch. 'Then why?'

He crossed his arms on the table and leaned on them. 'Deflection. He may not even realise it.'

It was so close to what she'd just been thinking she couldn't think of a thing to say. Nothing that wasn't dangerous. But Tony changed direction first, leaning back into the leather of the booth, the picture of relaxation.

'You should be flattered. I'm his favourite

brother; if he's letting me have you he must have a super high opinion of you.'

The arch look she threw him then should have stripped his skin. *'Letting* you have me? I hope you're joking.' The idea of someone giving her as a gift like that was as abhorrent as the thought that Sam might want to.

Tony laughed. 'He said you took no prisoners.'

Tired of the game, and feeling way more defensive than she was comfortable with, Aimee tried to turn the tables. 'He's married, Tony.'

A shadow flattened his eyes. 'I know.'

'So he wouldn't care one way or another what I do or who I do it with.'

He studied her. 'Do you believe that?'

'Don't you?'

'No. I see how he is with you. He cares.'

'Right. Enough to foist me off on his brother. *No offence.*'

'None taken.' He pressed his lips together. 'Maybe it's a way of keeping you close? Subconsciously?'

Her head-shake was immediate. 'He wouldn't do that to Melissa.'

Brown eyes turned nearly black. 'He's done worse to her.' But then they lightened a hint. 'And she's reciprocated, to be fair.'

There had been no hint of that a few days ago. She shook her head. 'He loves her.'

His eyes grew instantly keen. 'Did he say that?'

'Well, yes…' *Except*… She frowned. 'Actually, no. Not outright.'

He shrugged, as if that proved his point.

He mind whirled. 'Why would they stay together if they weren't happy?' Not that it was any of her business.

His eyes seemed to agree with that, but he eventually answered. 'Because of what it cost them. Neither one of them wants to throw that away.'

'What do you mean? What cost?'

Tony stared at her long and hard, deciding. 'Sam and I didn't speak for several years a while back.'

Years? Two brothers as close as this? 'Why?'

'Because of Melissa.'

Aimee flopped back into her seat. 'You were the brother she was friends with?'

'A lot more than friends.'

She internalised her gasp, but barely. 'He stole her from you? *Sam?*'

Tony's nostrils flared. 'Hard to know whether I should be flattered by your confidence in me or hacked off at your disloyalty to Sam. You think he was pitching out of his league?'

She ignored his attempt to redirect her and leaned in to match his brutal stare. 'Sam would never betray you like that.'

No question. Absolutely none.

The answer seemed to satisfy him. He relaxed. 'You're right. There's only one betrayer in our family and it isn't Sammy.'

'You loved her.' Aimee had felt enough shame

in her life to recognise it on sight. She sagged back into her seat. 'What did you do?'

And just like that the accuser became confessor. Suddenly his dark eyes looked a whole lot more like Sam's blue ones. 'Cheated on her. Dumped her after four years together. Sam willingly stepped in to fill the breach.'

She sucked in a stunned breath. 'He married her because you broke up with her?'

'He *dated* her because I broke up with her. He'd been waiting for his chance since his voice broke. He adored Melissa.'

'And then he married her.'

Tony's eyes fell. 'I beat the hell out of him. Three days before his wedding.'

Aimee couldn't help her shocked gasp.

'He could have taken me—he was so nimble and fast. But he didn't.' His voice thickened. 'He just let me pound him.'

Her heart squeezed for a young Sam who had loved his brother enough to allow that. 'Why?' she whispered.

The eyes that lifted reminded her of Coraline's. Filled with old, live pain. 'Because I needed to.' He swallowed hard and cleared his throat. 'He brought her down here not long after that. So it would be easier on her.'

Empathy surged from her aching heart and reached out to him, recognising its twin in suffering. 'Or maybe on you?'

He snorted. 'Or maybe on him. It doesn't

matter. All of that is in the past now.' His eyes blazed. 'All of it.'

He stared at her, and she had the distinct impression that he was trying to convince himself. And that she was missing something obvious. But before she could question him Sam appeared behind them, soundlessly.

'So, are there any secrets left?'

How much had he heard? On some instinctive level she knew that Tony had breached a trust by confiding in her. Made an exception for her. She wouldn't betray that—even if she didn't yet understand why he'd done it.

She fixed a light smile to her face and threw up her hands. 'Who knew you were such an ordinary child?'

'Ha ha!' Sam laughed thinly and slid in beside her. She wondered how long it would take her to be able to sit in a café booth alone without thinking of him.

Nothing she'd heard today changed anything. Sam's marriage might not be all roses but it was still a marriage. And if he was offloading her on his brother then he'd obviously decided where his loyalties lay. She struggled against the tightening of her face.

Sam's wary glance went from her to his brother. 'Everything okay?'

Aimee reached for her recorder and clicked it off. 'Sure,' she said, sliding it—and all its secrets—back into her handbag. 'We've just been getting to know one another.'

'You weren't kidding when you said she was bright.' Tony turned an appreciative smile on her.

Sam's gaze grew worried and ping-ponged between them.

You set us up, Sam! she wanted to shout. He could hardly protest at them getting along. Instead, she took a measure of satisfaction from matching Tony's warmth.

'You're very easy to talk to,' she said. Uncomplicated. Unconflicted. And un all the things his younger brother was.

But she'd still trade a dozen conversations with Tony for just one with Sam.

'I should get going,' Tony finally said, his voice still strained. Sam stood and they clutched forearms in brotherly farewell. Tony gently clapped him around the back of the head with his other hand. 'I'll see you next visit, Sammy.'

Then he reached down and took Aimee's hand in his and kissed the back softly. 'Lovely to meet you,' he murmured politely as he shot her a glance packed full of hidden meaning. *Don't hurt him.*

She inclined her head. 'And you.' *Understood.*

Sam's keen eyes saw it all.

Moments later it was just the two of them again. Just as it had been before Tornado Tony and his funnel of churning, swirling, baffling secrets had cut through her favourite riverside coffee shop.

And the hard conversation he'd interrupted

still needed to be finished. But she'd have to work her way back up to it.

'How often does he come to Hobart?' she asked casually, and Sam's eyes narrowed.

'Every couple of months.'

'What brings him here?'

He shrugged. 'Business. Why? Wanting to clear your diary for his next trip?'

She met his eyes head-on. 'You wanted us to meet.'

'I thought the two of you would…get along.'

'And we did.' In a tense, circling warriors kind of way. But beneath it all Tony struck her as someone she might come to like very much. 'He's a good looking man.'

But not a patch on his brother.

They were so similar, with a dozen key mannerisms in common. Both bright. Both articulate. Both brutally honest. And Tony *was* gorgeous— in a broody, damaged kind of way. Just ask the still dreamy-eyed waitress. Yet she'd felt nothing but curiosity when she'd looked in his eyes, nothing but warm breath when he'd kissed her hand, nothing but compassion when he'd spilled the secrets from their past.

So her attraction to his little brother clearly wasn't genetic. Or generic.

It was very, very specific.

Sam-specific.

So she owed it to herself to try one more time. To ask one more question before opting out of his life for good. To give them both a chance. She took a deep breath and leaned forward.

'Why did you come back early from Melbourne, Sam?'

There could only be two reasonable answers to that.

For my wife or *for you*. Either way, at least she would know.

She had no right in this world to hope or expect the latter, but if she never asked she'd never, ever know. And, as much as she believed the evidence of her eyes down by the river, she'd also believed the sincerity in his brother's voice when he spoke of Sam and Melissa together.

Sam's gaze grew guarded. 'I didn't.'

Aimee frowned. 'You must have.' To have been back in Hobart by noon, when their original flight hadn't been due to leave Melbourne until then.

Sam looked at her as if she was cognitively impaired. 'I came back on the original flight. Mel picked me up from the airport just after two. Why?'

She blinked at him, a cold suspicion washing over her. *Because that means it wasn't you I saw with your wife.*

She looked at the empty doorway through which Tony had departed and swallowed her dread. *Because that means you're being betrayed.*

'No reason,' she said, forcing lightness. Hiding her distraction. Her mind was furiously whirring as she scrabbled to know what the right thing to do was. The universe had just handed her everything she needed to end Sam's marriage. Her heart thumped under the burden of responsibility. 'Just making conversation.'

Sam looked at her oddly before he started filling her in on his last day of work in Melbourne. But the words only whooshed and buzzed in her head.

Melissa was cheating on Sam.

And it was Aimee's fault.

Sam's marriage was slipping away from him because he was too busy worrying about *her*. About *their* relationship. Never mind that it might have been slipping before he scrabbled down the side of the A10 and into her life a year ago, Aimee had felt responsible for it since they had met. If she hadn't been around he'd have picked up some kind of clue about a secret affair between his wife and his brother. He'd be taking action to prevent it.

She tried to look interested in whatever Sam was saying while her mind spiralled wildly.

'There's only one betrayer in this family and it isn't Sammy,' Tony had said, with dark eyes.

Present tense.

'You loved her,' Aimee had answered.

But maybe she should have used present tense, too.

'Are you okay?'

Aimee's attention snapped back to Sam from

the place where it had been drifting, out of focus. 'Sorry? What?'

'You kind of…zoned out.'

'I'm just…' She shook her head and sat up straighter in her side of the booth, looking every bit as distracted as she sounded. 'Sorry. What were you saying?'

Nice. She was away with the fairies while he was eating his heart out over the fact that, with Tony's help or without it, Aimee was leaving him. Today. He struggled not to let that frustration leak out as anger. None of this was her fault.

But he felt it as a seething, dormant kind of pain.

'I wasn't.' He studied her closely. 'We've been sitting here in silence for a couple of minutes. I've been watching you think.'

A flush chased up her throat. 'You should have…'

'Woken you sooner?' His smiled to take the sting out of his words and slid his hand over the table to cover hers, one finger curling under her palm. It practically burned into his skin. 'What's going on, Aimee? Why are you so determined to end our friendship?'

She took a deep breath, stared at their entwined hands. And she carefully extracted hers. 'You need to talk to your wife…'

His chest tightened. How many ways could he say it? And re-say it. 'We don't talk like this—'

'You *should* talk like this. With her. Not with me. You two need to talk about a lot of things.'

No doubt! Defensive heat surged up his neck. 'We're getting there.'

'Not fast enough.'

His gut dropped. If there was a way he could have everything he wanted didn't she think he'd take it? He pressed his lips together. 'You want out. I get that.'

I don't like it...but I get it.

Intensity surged green. 'I'm not good for you, Sam.'

'You *are* good for me.' The words tumbled out before he could think about the wisdom of uttering them. 'Seeing you is the highlight of my week. I can breathe when I'm with you.'

Her frown increased one more pained millimetre and her voice grew tight. 'That's what I mean. It shouldn't be that way.'

Frustration and panic struggled for dominance in the thumping of his heart. He wasn't used to being unable to control his fear, but none of his techniques were working. Was she working up to goodbye? 'You didn't cause my marriage difficulties. How is me not seeing you going to make things magically better with Melissa?'

'It will force you to focus your energies on your wife. Where they should be focussed.' His heart pounded as she straightened, reinforcing her lungs. 'I distract you, Sam.'

'You *save* me.'

The other patrons in the café paused in their conversations, their sipping, their clanking, and stared across the restaurant as the truth burst out of him like an accusation.

Aimee's eyes flared wide and dismayed.

He barely recognised his own voice: raw, tight. But he recognised the truth when he felt it. It sliced through him like a high tension wire.

He'd been in denial. All this time.

He'd dismissed it as friendship, he'd attributed it to the bond they had forged during the rescue, he'd dressed it up as an intellectual connection. Hell, he'd even set her up with Tony rather than see her walk from his life for good. How desperate was that? Even if his brother *was* the only man in the world he'd entrust her to.

Her eyes bled green pain across the innocuous café table. 'Don't you see how wrong that is?'

Shouldn't he trust his gut to tell him what was right and wrong? She didn't feel wrong. She felt very right. Which was why her judgement stung so much.

'I made a commitment to Melissa in front of family and God. And I will honour that commitment. I *am* honouring it.'

She tossed her head back, and her eyes were as scathing as he'd ever seen them. As judgemental. 'My father was fond of semantics when he wanted to be, too,' she spat.

Now? *Now* she chose to open up about her life?

'He justified cheating on my mother because he chose to do it within the marriage rather than leave her. How he must have patted himself on the back. *"I'm staying with Lis and the kid, I'll honour my commitment to them."'* Her chest heaved. 'What he never understood was that he should have been honouring *her*. Not just his legal obligation.'

It was only a glimpse into her life but it was an ugly one, and it reflected their present situation so keenly. The hurt in her eyes told him exactly how she felt about that part of her childhood, and how she likened it to what they were doing.

A dark shade crossed through him. 'I am not cheating on my wife.'

'Not physically.'

She might as well have booted him in the guts.

He thought back to the kite incident, to the many excuses he'd made to touch Aimee legitimately, or fire her up, to the burning desire to knock on her hotel room door that he'd only just managed to quash. Or—and his body reacted just as freshly now—to that one desperate kiss so many months ago that he'd never, ever forgotten.

But he fought the rising discomfort as though he was gasping for air. 'Not in any way.'

She leaned forward, one eyebrow arched. 'Does she know I exist?'

He stared, a numb anger burbling.

'No?' she challenged. 'Why not?'

Defensive heat swilled up and through him. He had no good answer. The anger-guilt threatened to spill over. But this was Aimee—kind-hearted, enchanting Aimee—not some hostile stranger. He floundered in her penetrating stare, silent. If he opened his mouth something bad was going to come out.

Bad for him. Bad for his marriage.

So he sat, rigid and silent in defiance of her inquisition.

But then her accusation softened, and she begged him with eyes rapidly filling with heartbreak, 'Why, Sam?'

Because it seemed wrong. It seemed like—

'Oh, my God...'

She pressed her hands flat on the table to steady them and blinked back tears. 'Do you understand?' she whispered.

The violent turbulence of long-ignored emotion raged inside him. He nodded. It was all he could manage past the painful wringing in his chest.

He wanted Aimee.

Not just physically—although he did. Not just emotionally—although he definitely did. He *wanted* her.

With him. Under him. Wrapped around him.

He'd betrayed Melissa in spirit, regardless of whether or not he'd touched another woman.

And he'd betrayed himself. The values he'd been raised with.

A smarter man would have recognised the signs. A stronger man would have walked away and stayed away. Smiled, shaken her hand and received his award, and then got the hell out of Aimee's orbit.

A better man would have seen this coming and done whatever it took to not let it happen.

'I won't be that woman, Sam.' *The other woman.* 'I watched my family be torn apart because my father couldn't honour my mother. I won't break up a marriage now.' He opened his mouth to protest but she raced on. 'And I won't be the woman that takes whatever emotional leftovers you can spare for me, either. I've done that my whole life.'

The moisture in her eyes wanted to spill over, but sheer willpower seemed to prevent it. Typical Aimee. A warm surge of admiration raced through him at her strength.

Don't appreciate it, Sam, a sardonic voice whispered. *She's walking out of your life.*

'I won't be the woman telling her life story to someone at eighty-five and bleeding pain on the page for the feelings she's kept hidden her whole lifetime. Or the woman who settles for near enough. I want it all, Sam. I'm worth it all.'

Determination blazed in her beautiful eyes, and it only emphasised those qualities of hers he felt such admiration for. Such a connection with. It only emphasised how much was missing from his marriage.

His gut tightened around a fist full of razorblades. 'Are you asking me to choose?'

Choosing Aimee would be an unforgivable betrayal of Melissa.

But choosing Melissa felt like an unforgivable betrayal of himself.

Her laugh dripped sorrow. *'I've* chosen, Sam. I'm walking away—'

'No…' His pulse practically shoved the word out of his mouth as it leapt into his throat. But of course she was. Of course she wouldn't hang around. She had too much dignity.

She clutched at her shirt-front. 'I'm worth more than pathetic grabs at whatever Sam-time I can get. Longing for something I'll never have. It hurts too much.'

Longing. Hurt. Those words spoke of so much more than just attraction. For the first time he looked inside her. Really looked. At the pain. At the dashed hope. At the—

He sucked in a breath and sat bolt upright.

She watched the moment the penny dropped with a furrowed brow. 'You moron,' she whispered, but it wasn't offensive. It reeked of self-derision and sorrow…and love.

And—finally—she laid herself bare before him.

Elation flooded his synapses, passed from blood-cell to blood-cell and pooled into his arid heart, shoving aside everything in its path. Melissa. His family. All the reasons he shouldn't be feeling like this. All the compromises and concessions he'd made over the past decade. None of that mattered.

Aimee Leigh loved him.

The best part of his world *loved him.*

But right behind the shot of pure adrenaline came a sobering chaser and his stomach twisted again. He'd been hurting her. She was hurting right now, under all that dignity and strength. He wanted more than life itself to be able to hold her hand. Ease her pain. Except that taking her hand would only cause her more pain.

Sorrow bled through him. How blind had he been not to understand that sooner?

Rational sense fled ahead of a surge of one-hundred-percent proof passion and gratitude and relief. He reached across the table and took her icy fingers in his, trusting the hurt would only be brief.

'Ask me.'

She lifted tired eyes. 'What?'

His whole future was concentrated in his intent gaze. 'Ask me to choose…'

He'd choose *her*. He recognised it like a light-ning-strike. He'd choose Aimee and he'd deal with whatever came. Melissa's broken heart. The condemnation of his family. He'd deserve it all, but he'd weather it with this woman by his side. This woman who filled him with joy and light. This woman who asked nothing of him but his kindness.

All these weeks, all these months since he'd first climbed into her car, she'd seeped into his soul like water soaking its way through a levy just before the whole thing exploded outwards from the subtle pressure, freeing a torrent into the valley below. *He* was that torrent, getting ready to burst.

Every part of him tightened up. 'Ask me now and I'm yours.'

She reeled back against the booth's cushioned supports and gave awful voice to a dry sob. It cracked out from between her ribs before she trapped it with a clenched fist to her lips.

People around them looked away awkwardly.

'No.' The word haemorrhaged out, tight and raw. 'I won't be the reason you end your marriage, or the reason you save it. I won't look into your eyes in ten years and see regret there for the decision of a heartbeat today, or wonder if you're working on a way to leave me, too.'

Shame sliced through him.

'I won't face your family knowing what they must think of me. Knowing what *I* think of me. Even if she—' She sucked her words back fast and thoroughly.

'Even if she what?'

Her eyes widened at whatever she wasn't saying. She took several deep breaths as he watched, waiting. 'You can't choose me. That's not who you are.'

Reality gnawed out from beneath all the euphoria and left him full of gaping ice-cold holes. No, he couldn't choose her—but not because he was a particularly good person.

Because *she* was.

His Aimee.

She leaned forward. 'Attend to your marriage, Sam. Save it or end it, but do it on your own terms. For your own reasons. Without me as a safety net or an excuse or a prize. Ask Melissa what *she* wants. You owe each other that.'

With all the dignity of a goddess, she scooped up her handbag, slid from the booth and walked away from him without a backward look.

He sat, his empty hands flaccid on the table, the sound of the cheerful little bell over the door taunting him as the woman of his heart walked out of his life without a further word.

And the levy broke.

Right. Left...

Getting her feet one in front of the other out through the door—out of Sam's life—was harder than walking across exposed nails. Every cell screamed at her to turn around, to run back into the coffee shop. But she pushed them onwards, ignoring the pain. Focussing on the pain.

She would keep putting right before left until she got to the car. Until she got home. While she packed her suitcase, loaded her laptop, locked her house, taxied to a travel agent and from there direct to the airport.

Because staying in Hobart was no longer an option.

Staying anywhere near Sam Gregory was not an option. She'd discovered hidden strengths that amazed her this year, but even those had their limit.

Ask me to choose.

Her chest compressed. The awful, excruciating irony.

She'd waited her whole life for a man who gave her options. Who asked instead of told. Who listened to her opinion rather than dictating what it should be. And the first time a man gave her the power over his choices…it was one she simply couldn't make.

Ask me to choose.

She never would. Because forcing Sam's hand like that would be unfair and wrong. But somewhere way deep down inside she so desperately wished he'd simply taken the initiative. That he'd made this one executive decision for her and demanded it rather than asking her to decide.

Because that was what *ask me to choose* really meant.

It meant *choose for me.*

And that was not a decision she was prepared to make. Even if—in the panic of that moment—he picked her. He wasn't free to. It wasn't practical for him to. He was committed to someone else, no matter how that someone else was treating him.

She reached the car park, crossed it, and fumbled her keys twice trying to get them into the lock. Just as she heard the *thunk* of her central locking deactivating she heard something else. A footfall right behind her.

'Aimee…'

She froze, her hand on her keys, her eyes falling shut, her back to him.

So close.

'You're right. I set this course years ago. I can't go back on it now.'

'I know.'

'She's a part of my family.'

'I understand.' Her eyes stared bleakly at the top of her car.

'And she's given me her life.'

Part of it. The temptation to tell him was so strong. She owed Melissa nothing. But she'd be destroying a brotherhood as well as a marriage if she did. And it would look for ever—to everyone—as if she'd done it to split them up. To get Sam for herself.

Loathing gnawed at her. Maybe that was what it was. Could she even trust her own motivation when she wanted him so very much?

So she just nodded her head once rather than risk speech.

'And you deserve more…' His breath practically heated her nape he was so close. Her skin prickled, aroused and desperate. She sucked in a tiny fraught breath and then held it to ward against him coming any closer. It felt like the last gasp she'd ever take.

'So much more than a man who isn't free to love you the way he wants to.'

Her chest tightened around the ball of pain that his words wrought and she braced her hands against the car for support. 'It's going to be hard,' she murmured, as a caution against either of them weakening.

He stepped an inch closer and she felt his chest

press against her back—as soft as a kiss yet as hard as tectonic force. 'It's going to be hell,' he murmured, right against her ear.

She swallowed against weakening, against leaning back into his strength, and curled her fingers around the rim of her car's roof to prevent her body from swaying unconsciously back into his.

It didn't work.

Between the beats of his heart and hers every part of her pressed into every part of him. Heartbreaking, sustaining, heaven. Hot, illicit torment. Then Sam was curling around her, twisting her in opposition, and he breathed a vow against her lips as they parted on a sob.

'If I'm going to hell, I'll go for a reason.'

The wet heat of his mouth forced a distressed gasp out of her.

So long. So very long between life-sustaining contacts.

His lips slid unrepentant and fatalistic across hers, coaxing them back to warmth. Back to existence. His arms tightened to steel bands and pressed her back into her open car door. But the discomfort barely registered as his mouth plundered hers. Forcing. Coaxing. Giving. Pleading silently for a response. Aimee's senses swam with delirious sensation and she sagged into his iron hold.

He deepened the kiss, lapping at her inside and out, breathing fire everywhere he roamed.

She dragged her hands upward, skirting over

the heat of his biceps, the hard curve of his shoulder, and then curled one around the base of his hot neck while the other anchored in his hair.

And she kissed him back.

Like champagne surging up the neck of a bottle, sensation rushed up her body and spurted out through the sensitive place where their mouths met. Her legs sagged and her inner muscles clenched. She'd been kissed before. Hard and fast. But nothing she'd ever experienced in her life had prepared her for a fully unleashed Sam. She hung onto him for dear life. The moment she reciprocated he ignited like a scrub-fire finding dry fuel, pressing her, worshipping her lips, drawing a moan from her throat. Echoing it and whispering in those bare moments that they sucked in a lungful of air.

'*Aimee…*'

He shifted and pressed into her from a new angle, the kiss softening, growing tender. Slower. As if he needed to ration the pleasure. He lapped at her lips, easing the kiss.

'Never forget this…' His murmured words seemed to come from his soul, not his vocal chords. Certainly that was where she registered them.

'You taste like for ever,' he breathed against her skin, and the beauty and awe in his voice helped her forgive him the fact he'd broken their last kiss to say it.

It *was* for ever.

That was how long it had to last them.

Sam pulled back so that he could stare down into her very heart and brushed a large thumb across her swollen lips. And then he whispered, 'Live your life, Aimee.'

He released her back against her car.

Then he turned and walked away. Without looking back. Without a goodbye. At least not a verbal one. Just as he had on the mountain.

The sight of those shoulders, hunched and hurt and hurrying stiffly away from her, would be the last she ever had of Sam Gregory. That and the feel of his mouth hot and blazing against hers. She surrendered to her weak legs and sagged down into her front seat, her trembling fingers going immediately to her mouth to trap the kiss there before it was lost.

'Live your life, Aimee.'

Her heart fractured in two pieces. He'd said that on the mountain, too. But back then she'd heard it as 'live *your* life' and she'd gone on to do that, to reinvent herself and make the beginnings of a new life outside the control of other people. She shuddered and sagged into her seat-back, the fabric pressing dangerously against the spikes of pain poking out of her. Could she do it again? She'd only had to push him out of her heart last time—now she needed to rend him completely from her soul. Visions of Cora and Dorothy and every other woman she'd interviewed floated before her. They had done it. In much harder circumstances than she was facing now.

'Live your life.' She'd heard Sam's words as

that this time. As in don't wait for him. Don't put her life on hold.

Live.

She could. She would. But how much of a life would it be without Sam to love?

She dropped her head forward onto the steering wheel of her car and tried very hard not to remember that that was how Sam had found her when he'd come into her life in the first place.

It was almost fitting that that was how he'd go out of it.

For ever.

CHAPTER TWELVE

As islands went, this one was pretty Australian. Aimee had thought about going overseas, somewhere tranquil and restorative like Bali, but in the end her need to put fast distance between Sam and her wavering conscience and her lack of current passport had made the decision easy. She'd searched instead for the furthest Australian point from Hobart. The north of the country technically qualified, but it was hot, humid country, and good girls from the south of Tasmania didn't do hot and humid, as a rule.

And so Perth it was—way over on the west coast of the country, perched on the edge of the Indian Ocean. But on arrival she'd discovered one place even further west than that—a tourist island about twenty kilometres offshore—and she'd made immediate arrangements to lease one of the very few long-stay tenancies available there. It was expensive, but what were savings for if not for funding sanctuary when you needed it most?

And sanctuary this most certainly was.

There were no private cars on Rottnest Island and only a handful of public ones. Everyone got around on bicycles or on foot or one of several lumbering buses circling the island, which made for a wonderfully slow and easy pace everywhere she went. There were more than sixty small bays on the island, and regardless of the fact it was the middle of winter Aimee visited a new one every day, slowly crossing them off like a geographic calendar to mark her time on the island.

Her old brick cottage with its wrap-around verandas sat high on a bluff and offered sweeping views to the mainland and over the hustling activity of the island's primary mooring and commercial centre. She'd built herself a pleasing ritual in the six weeks she'd been here: a wake-up coffee on the veranda first thing, then a slow stroll following her nose down to the old settlement and the bakery that pumped out the delicious aroma of freshly baked bread. She had a tray full of condiments to slap onto lavish, thick toast, after which she'd shower and then pick a bay to visit.

If it was on the blustery seaward side of the island she'd go in the morning and work in the afternoon, so that she didn't have to battle against the strong sea breeze on her rented bicycle. If it was on the less blowy west side she'd flip her schedule and work until lunch, then spend lazy hours exploring the new bay. Either way she'd then spend the long evenings working on her book.

She stood before her pinned-up map and tipped her head. Today…landward. She traced the long, skinny island's rocky shoreline with her index finger, looking for just the right bay. Her tracing halted on a tiny unnamed divot out at the southernmost point of the island, half hidden between two larger bays. Pleasingly inaccessible. The fourteen-kilometre round trip would be just taxing enough to give her a sense of achievement. She crossed it through with a black marker.

Twenty-two to go.

She'd promised herself she'd be recovered and ready to move on by the time she'd made her final cross on the map. And so far her soul was healing very nicely, thank you.

If scabbing over could be called healing.

This too shall pass. Coraline's last words to her had become her own personal anthem. Somewhere deep in her mind she'd decided that if she could just get through her time on the island she could move on and live her life without Sam. She just needed time.

The morning passed quickly as she finished transcribing the last of her recordings not related to Sam Gregory. She'd avoided those files, tucking them away safely on her laptop for another day. She'd even considered using a commercial transcription service to spare herself the pain, but knew that so much of the meaning was in the tone, in between the words, and that was the stuff that gave her oral histories their flavour.

That either made her highly professional or fatally masochistic.

But after lunch the tiny bay—and the hearty cycle out to it—did not disappoint. More rocks than anything, but despite the coolest day on Rottnest being a perfectly normal day in the south of Tasmania she wasn't interested in swimming, and so a good old-fashioned beachcomb through the rocks, dunes and crystal blue shore was a serene and restorative way to spend the afternoon.

So much so that as a squall came through in the evening she stoked up the fire in her trusty cottage, pulled a rug over her knees, filled a glass with a good Western Australian red wine and hovered her mouse over the folder called *'Sam 1.'*

She was ready.

It was time.

Her usual transcription process involved listening right the way through to get all the context and subtext locked away before she busied herself transcribing.

She clicked 'open.' And then 'play.' Then closed her eyes.

'So...'

Her own recorded voice was unnaturally loud in the silent little cottage, followed by the shuffling sounds of the digital recorder as she'd slid it across the table to Sam after the awards ceremony a lifetime ago.

'Tell me about your family. You're the oldest of...what was it...seven?'

She took a deep breath in the heartbeat that had passed between her asking and him answering. Then it came: his voice, rich and deep and relaxed.

'Eight. Second oldest.'

Her chest compressed immediately and her fingers tightened on the wine glass. It was like having him in the room with her. She could almost smell him. After so many weeks of absence her body reacted immediately—aching, hurting. She took a big swig of wine as she heard herself say casually, *'Big family.'*

Her mind saw the easy shrug of his shoulders as he'd answered. *'Lots of love to go around.'*

Sam talking about love was too excruciating. She missed whatever he said next as her heart rebelled and railed at her mind for putting it through such pain. The pride in his voice when he spoke of his family should have been a warning. A man with those kinds of family values would never leave his wife.

She took a series of deep breaths and tuned back in to her own voice asking him about his parents' example.

'Pretty tough act to follow?'

'I think we'd all consider it inspirational. Not demoralising.'

Except he considered it a whole lot more than inspirational. Their marriage was the bar against which he measured the success of his own. Two people for whom the marriage vows were more than just sacred, they were ingrained. Their

values were Sam's. They were the reason he
wouldn't leave Melissa, even if his for-better-or-
worse was two parts worse to one part better.

'You're protective of her.'

'Of course I am. She's my wife.'

His defensiveness hit her as strongly now, as
it had all those months before. He hadn't liked
his protectiveness being challenged. His carefully
built up defences.

'You love her.'

Again. *'She's my wife.'*

Aimee frowned. That wasn't a yes. She paused
and ran the digital file back a bit, listened to it
again with more volume. His voice had been
strained and curt, but he hadn't said yes. In fact
he'd never said it explicitly in all the recordings
she'd made and all the conversations they'd had.
He'd spoken of her intelligence, her goodness, her
gentle nature and his reluctance to hurt her.

But never love.

Yet he'd clearly loved her at the beginning.
Enough to marry her. Enough to leave his family.

That didn't change the fact that he'd chosen to
stay with Melissa now. But it killed her to imagine that he was condemning himself to a pas-
sionless marriage. A man who had the heat of a
volcano bubbling away inside him, just waiting
for a chance to erupt.

Her heart squeezed harder.

The recording went on as she remembered it.
Everything had got sticky right about then, and

she'd ended up calling a halt and bolting from the café.

She looked at her glass, which was suspiciously empty. She never drank while working—never—but this was an exception. This was too hard without a measure of Dutch courage.

A really healthy measure!

She double-clicked the file labelled *'Sam 2'* before pushing to her feet and padding across the cold floor in her woollen socks to the kitchen and the waiting bottle of red. *'Sam 2'* was the file from the ill-fated kite flying day.

They'd both grasped at the sanctuary her book offered rather than keep swinging away at each other's emotions. Any port in a storm.

She knew how this conversation started. She'd asked him to talk about how he'd first come to work in Search and Rescue. It had seemed safe after the tumultuousness of the conversations that came before it. And the kite flying. Her cottage filled with the sounds of the digital recorder clunking awkwardly to life and the noise of the café they'd sat in to record it.

Yet another restaurant. Yet another safe public place.

Red liquid tumbled high into her glass.

'Aimee...'

She fumbled the glass and sloshed wine all down her hand. Then she froze with her back to the laptop, to the warmth of the fire, staring out of the kitchen window into the swallowing darkness. As afraid to turn around as if Sam truly stood there.

That wasn't her voice.

'I'm recording this while you're in the bathroom...' He sighed, and it was so like the little groan he did while kissing it nearly undid her. Her knuckles tightened around the counter- edge. She still didn't turn around.

'I wanted to apologise again for today. The kites. I've been thinking while we walked back about why today happened.'

Her eyes fell closed.

'I can't honestly explain it. I only know that you energise me. You make me want to control time so I can slow it down when we're together and make it last longer. You make me smile and frown and roll my eyes with exasperation all at the same time.' Another sigh. *'But I like that. I want to teach you all those things your parents never did. I want to teach you about the world so that you are equal to it. You should never be less than you are capable of.'*

Aimee's hands curled so hard into the counter one of her nail-tips fractured. She peeled it off with trembling fingers, opened her eyes and locked them onto the darkness outside.

'It's awkward, this thing we have, but it's not insurmountable. We respect each other. We appreciate each other's mind. We're friends, Aimee. And that's a lot.' Dishes clanked in the background. *'That's something worthy—something to protect. I wish that I could have this conversation*

with you in person, but I get...' The longest pause
yet. *'...cloudy when you're here. The things I try
to say don't come out straight. But I know that at
some point you'll hear this and maybe you'll understand me a little bit better. You'll believe that
I have nothing but the best intentions in my heart.
And maybe we can talk about it then.'*

A guttural whimper escaped her tight lips. She
heard a raucous laugh that she remembered hear-
ing the first time, back in the café. Sam's voice
sped up.

*'You're coming back now. Whatever happens
in the future, Aimee...I want you to know you can
always count on me. I feel like I didn't finish rescuing you that day on the A10. I feel like there's
more I'm supposed to do.'* Pause. *'I hope you
smile when you hear this. At very least I hope
you don't cry. I'm yet to see you do that. I hope I
never do.'*

There was a clunk and a click and the recorder
went to the moment's silence it was programmed
to put between individual files. Then her own
voice filled the room again, bright and oblivious.

*'So, Sam... Tell me about how you came to be
involved with Search and Rescue...'*

But Aimee wasn't really listening. And she
certainly wasn't smiling. Sorrow too deep and
too perfect for tears surged through her body. She
stood half doubled over, clinging to the counter
as if it was the only thing holding her on earth.
Stopping her spiralling away into a vortex of
compounding pains. Was that what he'd meant

when he'd stood in the hallway in Melbourne and asked her if she was leaving because of what he'd said on the recorder? Did he think she'd listened to these words and never acknowledged them?

Let him pour out his heart and then just pretended they didn't exist?

'I feel like I didn't finish rescuing you that day on the A10.'

Her eyes squeezed shut.

Though she'd never heard them before, Sam's words summed up her own feelings so succinctly, so keenly, they cut her as surely as if they had been an actual blade. She'd worked hard on her independence—to own her actions and thoughts, to learn from her mistakes—yet here she was physically resonating with the truth of that simple statement.

Unless it was just plain old trembling?

Maybe there was no strength in being alone? Maybe true strength came from two people grasping each other? Like an arch. Immovable. Unbreakable. The strongest shape in nature.

But if they were the wrong two people… What then?

Sam's voice crooned on behind her, answering the questions she'd asked almost as a Band-Aid to the pain of earlier in the day, and his tone formed a reassuring blanket to drape over her hollowness. Still her knuckles whitened and the kitchen bench kept her from launching off into orbit and she determined not to move from that spot until she could be certain her legs would hold her.

CHAPTER THIRTEEN

TODAY was a no-work day. Sam's 'beyond the grave' message had thrown her so badly she'd tossed and turned and dreamed turbulent thoughts when she finally had got off to sleep.

The only silver lining was being up before the sun on what was the first really clear, warm day since the wet weather had set in. The glorious sunrise streaming in through her veranda doors made her think of fresh starts and new beginnings. It combined with the goodbye message from Sam—not that he'd meant it that way—and gave the beautiful day a strange kind of serenity. As if it was the first day of the rest of her life. An emotional turning point of sorts.

Not how she'd imagined or wished it would be, but not terrible either. Exactly as scary and exciting as the last time she'd done it, but definitely tinged with more sadness.

The strange mood made her restless. She picked the furthest bay to visit—a wild little point, far out to the blustery west of the island—

and on her return she still didn't feel like resuming work with her files. Or her book.

A day off. Something she'd not had since coming here.

And so here she was, as the afternoon wore on, curled up in a comfortable recliner in the window of a nearly empty coffee-house perched high on the edge of the island's main settlement, overlooking all the vacant moorings in the bay and the jetty where the ferries came and went like clockwork through the day.

She'd been sitting here long enough to see two come and go. And she knew from experience that the last ferry of the day would arrive at five p.m. and leave thirty minutes later. It was the off-season, so there wasn't a lot of traffic, but this late in the afternoon virtually all of it was outgoing. Tourists stretching their visit until the last possible moment and island staff heading home to their families on the mainland. Kids with bikes and surfers carrying their boards like guitar cases, families and couples, all waiting down on the jetty for the arriving passengers to disembark.

It didn't take long.

A group of five got off, all tiny in the distance. That was it. Her professional eye was drawn to the make-up of the group—a woman, two children and two men. Was it two families? One family and a friend?

The group paused after disembarking, turned, and the two largest of the speck-sized people shook hands. Then the family of four walked down the jetty towards their insignificant pile of luggage, leaving the other man standing there with his suitcase, lost.

Aimee stayed locked on the tiny speck as he wandered to the end of the pier and looked out to sea. Even the suitcase was incongruous. It branded him clearly as an out-of-stater. Locals bought backpacks, satchels, surfboards, boxes of food for their holiday. Few got off with suitcases. Even fewer on their own. On the last ferry of the day.

Then again, *she'd* disembarked alone. She'd had a suitcase.

Maybe this guy was as much an outsider as she?

The speck turned, looked up at all the businesses and accommodation lining the bluffs around the jetty, and started the long walk to shore and then up to the settlement. He carried his suitcase as if it was weightless.

Aimee's hand stilled on her coffee cup, halfway to her mouth, and hot liquid sloshed over the rim. His carriage. A man alone. Completely in opposition to the way people usually flowed on and off this island.

Sam?

She squinted and leaned closer to the glazed window. It could be. Or not. Maybe he was so firmly in her mind after the surprises and hurts of yesterday that she was seeing ghosts. Maybe he was just some random guy come to join his family after getting caught up at work?

But there was something about the sad way he strolled up the pier that hinted he had nowhere important to be. Or nowhere he was looking forward to going.

She stared as he got closer.

'Excuse me, miss?' A young waitress appeared beside her and held out a pair of binoculars. 'If you're looking for whales you'll need these. They most often surface around the southern corner of the island.' She pointed in the opposite direction.

Aimee wondered what the girl would think if she confessed she was watching a whole different kind of mammal. She took the binoculars and smiled. 'Thank you so much.'

As soon as the woman had returned to her work behind the counter Aimee swung around and pointed the glasses down to the jetty, searching amongst the trickle of people going out to the ferry for the only remaining passenger coming in.

And then she found him.

The breath she sucked in drew the attention of both staff behind the counter, and they glanced out of the window to the horizon to see what she'd seen. By the time they returned their focus to their work Aimee was on her feet, dropping the binoculars back onto the counter and heading for the door.

'Have a good day!' one of them called after her.

It was a long walk down to the jetty, even

at the pace she was going, but it gave her just enough time to moderate her instinctive flash of excitement, her mind-spinning amazement that he was here at all, her desperate panic that might miss him and then never find him again. It slowed her footsteps slightly.

She didn't want to look desperate. She didn't want to *feel* desperate. But since when did what she wanted ever have anything to do with reality?

She curved around the limestone retaining wall that raised the café high above the road sloping down to the jetty and darted her gaze left and right. Then she saw him, asking directions at the visitor centre on shore.

Her heart exploded into a painful thumping.

Sam.

She slowed her steps to nothing. Forced them to stop.

It suddenly seemed imperative that Sam's first sight of her should not be her rushing enthusiastically towards him. She'd done enough rushing towards him to last a lifetime. This time *he* had to come to *her.*

She stood, frozen, on the tarmac hill and waited for him to notice her.

His eyes were off to one side, studying the historic limestone buildings lining the shore, glancing up towards the bluff where her little cottage was dwarfed by one of the island's lighthouses.

Still she stood, unmoving.

See me.

His head whipped left as he swapped his case

to the other hand, looking down the long, clean beach that stretched until the island turned a corner, looking down towards the popular tavern on the shore, the rows of cottages the image of hers that lined the beachfront on the island's west end.

Still she didn't stir. Though it was one of the hardest things she'd ever not done.

See me, Sam.

He swung his gaze back to the roadway ahead and lurched to a standstill…and saw her.

He didn't move. Neither did she. Though her heart hammered wildly to be let out of its constricting cavity and fly to him. Then his feet started moving steadily, with purpose, and his eyes stayed locked on hers until she had to tilt her head to stare back into them.

The *thunk* could have been him dropping his suitcase at her feet, or it could have been the sound of her falling in love with him all over again. And undoing the good work of the past six weeks.

'Aimee.' Said with wonder. Said with pleasure. Said with infinite softness and sadness.

Sam.

He shook his head. 'I can't believe you're here.'

She frowned and her stomach sank. 'You weren't looking for me?'

His smile, so gentle and familiar, warmed the incredulous chill in her bones. 'I've flown to four different towns in the past two weeks looking for you. I meant I can't believe you're here, meeting me. How did you know?'

'I didn't know.' Or maybe she did. Maybe it was fate that had had her listen to that file last night. That had given her a spectacular day to force her outdoors and a spectacular dose of heartbreak to waste away the afternoon in this café. 'I was—' *spying on you with binoculars* '—passing. And then I saw you at the visitor centre.'

She could tell him the full truth later, once she'd discovered why he was here. If she was still able to speak to him.

'You saved me a difficult search. The island staff are particular about the privacy of their guests, it seems.'

Unlike her friends and family. 'Who told you where I was?'

'I flew up to your mother's place only to find you weren't there, then went back down to your father's. Your friend Danielle gave me a bum steer before finally taking pity on me and telling me where you actually were.'

Her lips tightened. So much for the solidarity of friends.

'Don't be angry, Aimee. She knew how hard I'd been trying. And she remembered me.'

'She's never met you.'

His eyes softened. 'She remembered me from your stories.'

Oh. She had been very effusive in her praise and appreciation after the accident.

'She said she owed me one for saving you that day. But now we're even.'

'How did you—?'

'I contacted every Danielle that the Department of Heritage has until I found her.' His lips twisted. 'There's fourteen, if you were wondering.'

She battled her body's instinctive reaction to his smile, the almost irresistible urge to lean into it.

'She also asked me to tell you that the McKinley tapes are ready.'

The McKinley tapes. Their workplace e-mail code whenever one of them wanted the other to call them urgently to talk. When something exciting was up. Yes, the McKinley tapes were almost certainly ready to burst!

'Thank you.'

The island reeled around her. That she was standing here, making such smalltalk with Sam...

Sam!

She shook her head at the inconceivability of it.

'Is there somewhere we can go to talk properly?' he asked, reading her expression.

Her eyes flicked up to the bluff, to her warm little cottage. But taking him into her space didn't feel like the best decision ever. It was hard enough having him in her house in spirit...

'There's a café just here.'

To their credit, and Aimee's undying gratitude,

the two staff masked their surprise at her return and treated her as if they hadn't seen her run out of there just a few minutes before. They showed her to the same table and took a speedy order.

Aimee tucked her hands under her thighs and lifted her eyes to his. 'Why are you here, Sam?'

'I came to find you.'

'Why?'

'Because I don't like how we left things. In Hobart. I didn't know you'd gone.'

The subtext was clear. *You should have told me.* Old sensitivities bristled. From way before Sam. 'I wasn't aware I had to lodge an itinerary with you.'

He winced. 'I was worried about you. You just disappeared.'

Even her shrug was defensive. 'I might have been ignoring your calls.'

'I'm sure you were. You blocked my e-mails.'

She dropped her eyes at that little bit of immaturity. She'd been so desperate to close off any avenue back to him. A self-preservation thing. She couldn't trust herself not to weaken.

'I went to your apartment,' he persisted. 'It was all locked up and your neighbours told me they were collecting your mail and watering your plants.'

'So clearly I wasn't dead.'

'I wasn't worried that you'd done something, Aimee. I was worried that you were alone somewhere. Toughing it out. And I couldn't help you.'

'How exactly did you imagine you appearing was going to help?' *Is* going to help.

'Things got…out of hand that day. I wanted to apologise. To make sure you were okay.'

'Chivalrous to the end. Well, you've found me.' She held her hands up and indicated around them. 'Happy in paradise.'

'You don't look very happy.'

'On the contrary. I've found a real…peace here. It's helped me to get a lot of things straight in my head.'

Creases appeared between those expressive brows. 'What kind of things?'

'My future. What I want from life.' She straightened. 'What I don't want.'

'Sounds like you've had a productive holiday.'

'This isn't a holiday. I'm working.'

'On the book?'

She nodded. 'Amongst other things.'

'How's it going?'

'You came all this way to talk about my book?'

He stared at her. Shook his head. 'Did I do this to you, Aimee?'

Her heart whomped hard. 'This?'

'This sarcasm. The defensiveness. It's not you.'

'Maybe this was always me. We didn't exactly part on the best of terms.' If you didn't count the public display of more than affection.

'No, but… Through everything you were always so…gentle.'

Her laugh was everything but. 'If I seem harsh it's because I'm protecting myself, Sam.

It's not easy seeing you.' He glanced out to sea and then dragged his eyes back, as though facing her pain like a man was the punishment he was due. 'You've had weeks to get used to the idea of seeing me. I've had minutes. Give me a break.'

'I'm sorry. You're right.'

He smiled as the waitress slid two steaming cups onto the table, though it was hollow. Pretty much exactly how Aimee felt. She was full of the joy of seeing him again but she wasn't letting any of it out.

'Drinking coffee is all we seem to do,' he said.

'We always were particularly talented at finding legitimate ways of spending time together.'

They fell to silence. It was a far cry from the comfortable ones they'd used to share.

Her mind made the obvious leap. 'How is Melissa?'

He frowned and seemed to pick his words carefully. 'She's good. Really good.'

That hurt—why wouldn't she be good? She had the best man in the world fighting for her—but she watched him closely for his next reaction. 'And Tony?'

He flicked his eyes up, surprised, but gave nothing else away. 'He hasn't been back since you met him. But he's well.'

So Tony was off the scene and things were 'good' with Melissa. It was what Sam wanted. But it was hard to be pleased for him. Even with the benefit of six weeks of emotional distance. Those weeks had counted for nothing the moment she saw him standing on the jetty.

Her eyes followed that thought. 'Your ferry's leaving.'

He didn't take his eyes off her. 'I don't care.'

'It's the last ferry of the day.'

'I'll sleep on the beach if I have to.'

'It's the middle of winter, Sam.'

He shrugged. 'I'm rugged. And survival trained.'

She glanced at her watch. If he didn't get a cottage then she'd have no option but to offer him her sofa. 'If we hurry we'll catch the visitor centre before it closes. There's plenty of empty cottages on the island.'

'This doesn't strike me as an island that hurries anything. Finish your coffee. Tell me what you've been doing for the past six weeks.'

She pressed her lips together and drank as fast as the heat of her coffee would allow, and tried not to get annoyed at how he took his time. 'You're stalling.'

'I'm relaxing. It's been a hard couple of weeks.'

Tell me about it.

But eventually he finished up and they paid, and walked back down to the waterside visitors' centre. Just in time to see the shutters going up.

Her eyes squeezed shut.

Great.

'Got a plan B?' Sam said casually.

'Closed at 5.30p.m.' There was an enormous

notice next to the counter that advised customers. Sam had to have seen it when he'd popped his head in here before. An urge to be contrary overwhelmed her. 'I'll give you an extra blanket. You're going to need it down on the beach, GI Joe.'

Sam smiled at her churlishness. 'Great. Let's go get it. I'll walk with you.'

Aimee turned and stalked ahead of him back up the road, then threw a right at the top and trod the familiar path around the edge of the bluff. Sam lagged, studying the barred heritage buildings from a century before when the island had been a penal colony.

'This reminds me of Hobart,' he said, calling ahead to her. 'Except warmer.'

Maybe that was why she felt so at home here. She slowed and let him catch up. They walked past the budget family accommodation, where the smell of early dinners for children wafted around them and bright, inviting lights blazed in old fashioned windows. Eventually she was wiping her feet on the doormat to her cottage as Sam clunked up the timber steps behind her.

'I'll just get you that blanket.'

He fired his baby-blues at her. 'Seriously, Aimee? You're not going to ask me in?'

Of course this had always been his plan, and of course she'd seen it coming. But had it not occurred to him that this was the first time they'd been together behind a closed door alone *ever*?

It sure as heck had occurred to her.

An isolated cottage high on the bluff of an island was neither public nor safe. And it really wasn't somewhere that a married man should be with the woman he'd kissed half to death the last time they saw each other. But she could hardly throw him out.

Ugh! She pushed through her front door and let it swing wide behind her.

Into the breach…

'Wow. Look at that view.' The lights of the expansive capital of Western Australia twinkled in the distance across twenty kilometres of darkening ocean as the winter sun slunk down over the island behind them. 'I can see why you call this paradise.'

'It *was*…' she muttered, and left it hanging. She crossed to the fireplace and started to lay her evening fire.

He didn't offer to help, he just helped. And he didn't take over, either, like every man she'd ever known would have. He just anticipated her fire-making process and was ready with what she needed next. Kindling. Rolled up newspaper. Firestarters. Matches.

Within minutes the house crackled with the pop and hiss of a young fire just getting going.

Aimee walked into the kitchen and yanked the cork from the bottle of red sitting on the counter, then poured a liberal dose into the waiting glass. She held up an empty one in his direction.

He shook his head. 'No, thank you.'

Suit yourself. 'What?' she finally said when she noticed his quizzical expression.

'I've just realised I've never seen you drink alcohol.'

'Worried you've driven me to it?'

His tiny smile hurt her heart. 'No. But it's a reminder of how little we actually know about each other.'

She took a deep breath to smother the bite of pain that statement generated. 'Just as well you're not staying, then.'

He leaned on the old timber fireplace surround and eyeballed her. 'If you want me to go, Aimee, just say the word. I didn't come here to upset you. I just wanted to say my piece.'

'It upsets me. Naturally it does. I came a long way to try and restore some equilibrium. You've shattered it.' She waved at the cosy cottage features around them. 'Even this place will now remind me of you. My sanctuary.'

He dropped his head.

'But done is done. Say your piece and go. I'll go back to rebuilding my life. Although I really can't think of anything we left unsaid the last time we spoke.'

She crossed her arms and leaned on the far counter, the timber kitchen island strategically positioned between them.

His eyes burned into hers even across the room. As if there was something he really wanted to say but couldn't bring himself to. 'Back in the car wreck last year, you told me a story about

Dorothy, the woman who came out here as a teen and moved to the gold fields with a man she barely knew. How she stayed when she was terrified and miserable because she wanted to honour her commitment.'

It was a question, even if it didn't sound like one. 'I remember.'

'The way you spoke that night, and things you've said since…about your father… They led me to believe that you rate personal integrity highly. That you feel honouring a commitment is a worthy trait.'

She nodded.

'So why do I feel like you're disappointed in me for honouring my commitment to Melissa and persevering with my marriage? Like you're condemning me for it?'

It didn't surprise her that he'd picked up on it. It was exactly the complicated paradox she struggled with daily. 'Respecting your values and liking them aren't the same thing.'

'Would you have me do less?'

Would she? A man like Sam being free and easy with someone else's emotions? She shook her head.

'Yet it's still there in your eyes—the disappointment. Even now.'

'It's not disappointment. It's—' She averted her eyes for fear of what else he might see in them and changed tack. 'It wasn't like I didn't have fair warning. You told me back on the mountainside that you never started something without finishing it. On principle. Your marriage is no different.' It hurt to say it but she owed him the truth. 'I do admire your determination to make your marriage work.'

'But?'

But I hate it. She risked a direct stare. 'But I think you've made a mistake.'

Not what he was expecting her to say, judging by the fold in his brow. 'How?'

Because Melissa isn't working nearly as hard to honour your marriage as you are. Could she tell him that? Could she trust her subconscious not to be spitting it up intentionally to come between Sam and his wife? She hedged. 'What if you're not meant to be together? What if that's what you were supposed to take from all of this?'

What if the lesson she was supposed to take from Cora's story was that she should be fighting for what she wanted rather than just walking away? It had only taken an hour back in his company for her to know—without any doubt at all—that a life with Sam was what she wanted. More than anything.

'Then my mistake was made ten years ago, marrying Mel. It wouldn't really be honour if I only called on it when things were going well.'

His words fitted almost perfectly with her own values. Yet she abhorred them. Her throat thickened. 'What if I'm the person you're supposed to be with?' It was tiny and raw and the most honest thing she'd ever said to him. Possibly to anyone—including herself.

The wind battered against the window frame and his body stiffened in front of her as if he expected it to burst in and start buffeting him, too.

'You think I haven't asked myself that?' he murmured over the noise of evening closing in. 'Every time we were together having such a good time? Every time we laughed at the same corny joke? That maybe Mel and I weren't supposed to be together? My own disloyalty made me sick even as I was craving more time with you.' He ran expressive fingers through his hair. 'But then I started in on the blame game. Maybe I'd choked my marriage in trying too hard to take care of her? Maybe our inability to talk was my fault? Maybe being drawn to a fresh, bright new toy was just the coward's way of ending the relationship? And I ended up doubting that I had any honour at all.'

She stared at him.

'I used you, Aimee. I drew you in to my problems and then set you up as an excuse to avoid dealing with them. I indulged the attraction between us and I made a hundred excuses for why. I kissed you when I knew a clean break would be easier for you.' He took a breath. 'I have no more excuses now. I'm just so very sorry. That's what I came here wanting to say.'

Her heart squeezed up into her tight throat. Had she honestly expected more? 'Why are you saying it now?'

'There are things I wasn't free to say before.'

Before... The stream of thick blood powering

her pulse pushed harder against her artery walls. Her eyes instinctively went to his hand before she remembered that was not where he wore his wedding ring. They flicked to the spot below his throat instead. Tan fingers flipped the top button of his shirt and drew out the leather thong.

Absent of ring.

'Melissa and I have split up.'

A hole torn open in the planet's atmosphere right above the cottage, and all the oxygen fled Aimee's cells in a rush. She gasped for air she was sure wasn't there. If not for the sturdy counter behind her, her legs would have crumpled under the force of her shock.

He was free.

Her mind spun with a wild mix of vertigo and delirium.

He was free and he was *here.*

Blind hope she didn't dare give voice to crashed headlong into a wounded kind of fury. She exhaled, and feared the crush of emotion would stop her being able to breathe in again. 'What? You were just hoarding that fact close to your chest, like a prize? You've been here an hour, Sam!'

He was with her in a heartbeat, gently removing the glass from her trembling fingers and steering her to the sofa in front of the barely warm fire. 'You seemed so strong. You said you were fine…at peace. I had to be sure, Aimee. The way we left things you'd have been well within your rights to throw me that blanket and slam the door in my face.'

Fury swilled around her. The hour he'd kept that secret felt as long and painful as the weeks that had gone before it. 'That's still an option,' she gritted.

He twisted on the sofa to face her. 'Your strength mocked me. It showed me what a coward I'd been in not addressing things with Melissa openly. I'd been so concerned about hurting her, about ripping her foundations out from under her...'

What did you do? The words swam around her mind but refused to get in order on her tongue.

'But I was doing it for me, too. She'd been a part of my family for so long—a beloved daughter. I couldn't bear to imagine the look on my family's face when I came home at Christmas without her. I was her connection to them.' His eyes greyed over. 'But turns out I was her connection to something else. Some*one* else.'

'Anthony.' She barely whispered the name.

He stared at her, disorientated. 'You knew?'

'I was terrified if I told you it would be because deep down I wanted to come between you. Or that you would think it was that.' She lifted her eyes. 'He loves her.'

Sam dropped his head. 'He always has.'

His distress showed in the several places on his face that he didn't quite master. Empathy washed through her. For no reason she thought of Charley McMahon. She'd spent so long thinking about how Cora had lost her Danny she hadn't thought about Charley losing his only brother, too. Was this the end of Sam's relationship with Tony as well as Melissa? How badly was he hurting right now?

'But so do you,' she whispered.

He pushed to his feet, crossed to the fire, prodded it to flame and then dropped a large piece of karri onto it. 'Not like he does.'

She stared at him, the blood slowly returning to her face in warm tingles. 'You married her.'

He turned back, let his tongue worry his lip for a moment, then met her confusion with steady eyes. 'Melissa had been with Tony since she was thirteen, and I'd had a thing for her for most of that. She was smart and gentle and so pretty—and I was just brimming over with undirected adolescent angst. I was enraged when he broke it off with her—for her, that he could be such an ass—and embarrassed that someone from my family had done that to her. So I took my chance.'

He sighed.

'We started hanging out, then making out, then going out…And she got to stay with the people who loved her. After a few years there was a lot of pressure on us both to make a decision. The idea of breaking up with her after so long…'

'You couldn't do it.'

'One Gregory had already trashed her heart. I couldn't do it twice. Plus I honestly believed I loved her. I didn't look hard at all the reasons it wasn't the best idea.' He sank down next to her on the sofa. 'That was a bad call. For both of us.'

'It wasn't love?'

'I adore Mel. She's a brilliant scientist and a wonderful woman. But…' His eyes dropped. 'She wasn't mine to rescue. All the passion in our relationship came from my elation at finally having her for myself, and that eventually waned. By then I'd stopped looking at the signs it wasn't working. I just became determined that it would. For her sake.'

'She didn't love you either?'

'She never stopped loving Tony.'

A rush of sensation raced across her skin. Just like Cora and Danny. But Sam might have been the younger brother destined to live his life with a woman who never really loved him.

'Why did she stay?'

He snorted. 'We were as deluded as each other. Melissa felt like she'd used me—like *she* owed *me* something. And I had nothing to compare it to until…'

His eyes narrowed with the struggle to verbalise something.

'Until?'

He twisted further on the sofa and took both her chilled hands in his furnace hot ones. 'Until some crazy lady in a Honda just about took out my eardrums with the horn of her car one freezing night on the A10.'

She clenched her fingers around his to stop their tremor.

'One night, Aimee. We had just those few hours together and yet the memory of you troubled me more than I could understand. The connection I couldn't fathom. It killed me to see the disdain on your face as you walked across that stage in Canberra—'

'I was angry. You had a wife. And you let me…' *Fall for you. Overnight.* She pressed her lips closed.

'It doesn't matter. But as I stood there in my too-tight suit and you slipped your arms around my neck…that was like going home for me. The most perfect thing I'd ever felt. And I knew right then that my marriage was over. I just didn't want to acknowledge it.'

'I never wanted to be the reason you split.'

'I'm the reason we split. And Mel. She'd stalled me for years on the subject of kids. Now I know why. When we finally spoke it was like a tsunami of repressed feelings—a decade's worth. All so misguided and pointless. If we'd gone on much longer they would have turned hostile.'

'Ten years is already a long time.'

'It was turning thirty that did it for her. She realised she was going to grow old and die with a man she didn't love. All because she didn't want to hurt him.'

Shades of Coraline again. 'She didn't love you? Not at all?'

He thought about that. 'We care for each other deeply. Enough to know when to call it a day.'

She stared, her heart beating stronger and faster. 'And she's with Tony now?'

'She always was in her heart.'

'Will that bother you? Them being together?'

The left side of his mouth twitched. 'Not nearly as much as it's going to bother him knowing I slept with his wife.'

The comic image of a simmering Tony sitting across the dinner table from an irascible Sam with Melissa in the room even made *her* smile. Just a little bit.

'They're getting married?'

'I hope so. As soon as the divorce is finalised.'

More silence fell.

'I won't lie to you, Aimee. It wasn't a fun few days. I had to face some stuff in my life that I… Things I've done that I'm not super proud of. My original withdrawal from our marriage hurt her. I was the connection to the people that she loved—to Tony—and I used that to keep her kind of an emotional hostage. I think, without knowing it, I was punishing her for not being…perfect. I wanted the perfect marriage. The perfect love.'

He'd called *her* perfect just a moment ago.

'Like your parents?' she said. His head barely bobbed. 'What do they think about all of this?'

'They want us to be happy. All of us. It's weird for them, of course, but they barely need to do anything more than change the labels on our Christmas stockings. I imagine we'll have some awkward name slip-ups for the first few months…'

She stared at him. For eternity. The log showered loud sparks in the fireplace. 'So you're free.'

His eyes practically glowed as they fixed on hers. 'I'm free.'

'What will you do?'

Blue fire blazed down onto her. 'That depends on you.'

'Are you assuming that your marriage status is the only thing stopping me from being with you?'

'Uh…' That halted the blue fire. His gaze grew guarded. 'I kind of was. Yes.'

'No. There's something missing.'

'Missing? Between us?'

Aimee took a deep breath. 'You've spent the last half-hour telling me about the love you *don't* feel for your wife, the love that she *does* feel for Tony…'

The bemusement on his face would have made her smile if this wasn't so serious. This was the rest of their lives.

'Right…?'

'What about me?'

He shifted closer, gave her *the look*. 'You know how I feel about you.'

'No, Sam. I don't. We've never been able to acknowledge it. I know you're attracted to me, but that's not enough to change our lives for.'

'You want the words?'

'That's all I've ever wanted.' And in a flash she realised that was true. 'I want a man with character and integrity. A man who's compassionate but fearless.' Her heart tightened into a fist. 'Someone who's confident enough in himself to let me be in charge sometimes.'

'That's quite a wish-list.'

'I met a man on a mountain once who had all of those qualities.'

His eyes darkened with confusion. 'Anything else?'

She'd come this far. She wasn't backing away now. 'Yes. A good man who loves and respects me and isn't afraid to say it publicly.'

He stared at her long and hard. Then he got up and walked out of the room.

Aimee blinked, stared at the door expectantly. Waited for the return that didn't come. Then on an angry curse she launched to her feet and shot off after him, grabbing her scarf on her way out through the door.

When she got outside he was halfway up the hill to the lighthouse at the tip of the bluff. Rapidly disappearing into the shadows.

A sick hollowness weighed her down, and she pulled the scarf tighter around her shoulders. Had she asked for too much? More than he was prepared to give? More than he was capable of giving?

But, no. Asking for what she wanted was not a bad thing in her new life. And expecting Sam's love was not unreasonable. If he couldn't offer that… Well, then she would be no worse off than she had been this morning, staring at the sunrise and thinking about the promise of a solo future ahead of her.

Except that she would. How could a future without Sam possibly be as bright as one with him? But she wouldn't run after him this time.

She stopped. Turned for the house.

And then she heard it. Muted and buffeted by the night winds.

'Sam Gregory loves Aimee Leigh.'

She froze. Frowned. Turned back to look up to the lighthouse.

A tall shadow stood at the base of the building, his arms stretched out to the endless black ocean, throwing his voice to the heavens. Throwing his heart open to the heavens.

'Sam Gregory loves and respects Aimee Leigh!' This time louder, clearer, as the wind dropped.

Her breath caught.

The shadow turned and jogged down off the lighthouse's paved base, across the turf and back onto the road leading to her cottage. He didn't stop until he got to her.

'I will never tire of saying it publicly,' Sam vowed. 'But let me say it privately...'

He snagged both ends of her scarf and pulled her into his body, twisting the fabric ends in his fists and holding her tight against him. 'I love you, Aimee. I've loved you since the moment you gave me your trust on that mountainside. So distracted by your courage and strength I made rookie mistakes all night. Not being able to acknowledge it, not being able to acknowledge *you,* is a hell I don't ever want to repeat.'

She stared up at him. 'You love me?'

'I honour you. And I *choose* you.'

Tears prickled and spilled over

'Aimee...' He wiped at them, both sides, with his thumbs, frowning. 'You never cry.'

She laughed, watery and sniffly. 'I do now.' She stretched up and wrapped her arms around his neck. 'I love you so much, Sam.'

And then his lips were on hers, gentle and questioning, as his large hands framed her face. She kissed him back fiercely, determined to show him that she wasn't just accepting him because he was offering, to show him how much she wanted him. How much she loved him.

How strong she was without him but how much stronger she was with him.

'Your nose is freezing,' he murmured, and she nuzzled it into the warmth of his beautiful neck, amazed and awed to know that she could do that every day for the rest of their lives if she wanted. And of course she did.

'Let's get you inside,' he said, tucking her under his arm. 'There's a sofa in front of a fire in there that I'm just dying to stretch out on.'

'You don't really have to sleep on the sofa.' She laughed.

He nudged her sideways as they walked, entwined, his voice rich with promise. 'I have no intention of sleeping on it.'

* * * * *

A sneaky peek at next month...

RIVA™

LIVE LIFE TO THE FULL – GIVE IN TO TEMPTATION

My wish list for next month's titles...

In stores from 6th April 2012:

❏ Cracking the Dating Code – Kelly Hunter

❏ New York's Finest Rebel – Trish Wylie

❏ The Fiancée Fiasco – Jackie Braun

Available at WHSmith, Tesco, Asda, Eason, Amazon and Apple

Just can't wait?

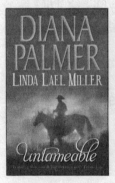

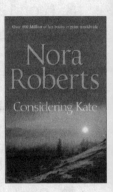

Have Your Say

You've just finished your book.
So what did you think?

We'd love to hear your thoughts on our
'Have your say' online panel
www.millsandboon.co.uk/haveyoursay

- 🌹 Easy to use
- 🌹 Short questionnaire
- 🌹 Chance to win Mills & Boon® goodies

Visit us Online

Tell us what you thought of this book now at
www.millsandboon.co.uk/haveyoursay

YOUR_SAY